A NEW BEGINNING

A second chance in life...

a novel

JORGE A MAZZA

2020 Revised English Edition

This is a work of fiction. Names, characters, places, and incidents are the products of the author's imagination or are used fictitiously. Any resemblance to actual events, locales, or persons, living or dead, is entirely coincidental. Reincarnation, as presented in this book, doesn't correspond to beliefs taught by religions such as Hinduism and Buddhism.

Title: A New Beginning / Jorge A Mazza
Description: 2020 English Edition.
Identifiers: ISBN (e-book): 978-1-7770845-0-9 | ISBN (5.25 x 8 paperback): 978-1-7770845-1-6

A NEW BEGINNING

A second chance in life...

Cast of Primary Characters

Alfredo: The innocent youngster reincarnated and sharing consciousness with **Raul Rivera Paez**

Susana: Raul's wife

Valeria and **Maria Jose:** Raul and Susana daughters

Analia: Alfredo's first wife

Paola: Alfredo's fiance.

Ricardo: the young cult follower reincarnated by **Norberto:** the corrupt union leader

Virginia: Ricardo's wife

Irene: obsessive compulsive teacher reincarnated by **Isabel:** the free spirited youngster

Felipe: Irene's husband

Mike and **Anton:** the homosexual couple

Diana: the shy secretary reincarnated by the theatrical Sandra

Santiago: Diana's husband

Chapter 1

"I have come to cast fire on the earth."
(Luke 12, 49-53)

Raúl left the court in triumph, having won one of the most famous and public trials of recent times; the divorce of a well-known young actress from her unfaithful husband—a wealthy industrialist considerably older than her.

Raúl Rivera Páez, a young and brilliant lawyer, had worked his way up in his law firm in a very short time, and was now a partner in one of the most prestigious law firms of Buenos Aires. Of course, this came with a commensurate increase in his salary, with which he and his wife Susana could indulge their extravagant tastes: vacations in Europe, clothes by famous designers, jewelry, domestic service for all their needs, a German car for him and for Susana, an immense apartment in Récoleta with a double garage, and decorated with the most expensive furniture in the market, as well as a house in the country for the weekends.

His last name, Rivera Páez, apparently came with aristocratic associations, but he never explained its origin.

On the contrary, he preferred others to believe that he belonged to a traditional family. At least he knew that his surname was not linked to any great fortunes or prestige; indeed, his paternal grandfather had escaped from the north of Spain like thousands of other emigrants, attracted by the promise of a better future than Galicia, the poorest region of the Peninsula, could offer.

. . .

His grandfather Nicanor had arrived in Buenos Aires aboard a cargo ship knowing he would never return. He knew he would never see his family again—and he didn't care. Crossing the ocean at the age of seventeen, being the youngest, he had suffered hardship and abuse from the rest of the crew. They made him work without sleep and gave him a ration of food so small that he lost ten kilos in the crossing—even though it was not noticeable because of his thick bone framework.

Arriving in Buenos Aires with a small bag of clothes as his only belongings, walking to the central train station a few blocks from the port, Nicanor was amazed by the crowds of people moving in all directions, and by buildings taller than he had never seen. Despite his youth and the fact that he had never been to a big city, he didn't feel out of place here. He wanted to forget everything he had left behind. While in Spain, he had been told about the immensity of the Argentine countryside, with job opportunities even for someone like him with little or no experience.

He bought a ticket that took him to Trenque Lauquen, a small town about 400 kilometers from Buenos Aires in the middle of the fertile wet pampas. The center of town had a few blocks of poor flat houses—all of them a worn cream color—separated by streets made of a mixture of earth and stones that became impassable with the slightest rain. As small as it was, it had the typical central square. The grass in the middle of the summer was dry and neglected, and there were a few wooden benches well-used by the seniors during the day and by the lovers at dusk.

In the center of the square, there stood a bronze monument of some hero mounted on horseback. No one remembered his name or what he had done to deserve a statue, but his extended right hand, as if ordering his soldiers to get ready to kill, suggested that he had fought against the indigenous people during the tragic desert campaign. Now the outstretched arm only served the pigeons that gathered to perch, leaving greenish-brown excrement as sad decorations that only the heavy rains could clean.

The village was surrounded by 500,000 hectares of very fertile black land where wheat and cattle flourished naturally, almost effortlessly. As in the interior of all these small towns in the countryside, on one side of the square was a church with a tall bell that rang to announce special events, such as funerals, weddings and the beginning of the Masses. On the other side was the municipal building that could be seen everywhere because, at three stories, it was the tallest in the town. In front of the square there was a confectionery where well-appointed women had tea with delicious cakes. In the summer, protected by an awning, they sat at tables in the sidewalk where they could see what was going on in the square. They were the wives of the school principal, the lawyer, the doctor, the dentist, and some ranch owners. The most important activity was to gossip about anyone who was not sitting with them at that moment. There was not much else to do in Trenque Lauquen.

Opposite the confectionery, on the other side of the square, there was a dismal bar nearly always occupied by the village drunks, who played cards in addition to endless drinking. There was also a billiard table with a torn green cloth where the youngest practiced for hours on end.

The obligatory weekend ritual for the young people of Trenque Lauquen was to stroll endlessly around the square—boys in one direction, girls in the other. It was their opportunity for an exchange of glances, often months before they dared to speak.

On his first day at Trenque Lauquen, Nicanor toured the town tirelessly in search of work, offering himself as a laborer or for whatever work he could find that would get him a place to stay, something to eat, and with luck, a small salary that he intended to save in full.

The first few nights, he huddled under a bench in the plaza. At least it was summer, and he could sleep in the open, despite the mosquitoes that tortured him. He soon got work at one of the local ranches under the supervision of a foreman who seemed to be drunk most of the time. He shared a dirty mud-walled ranch house with three or four other laborers to whom he rarely spoke. Each had a cot with a straw mattress used by many generations of workers before them, and probably also a few stray dogs.

Nicanor was taller than most boys his age, had a leonine face and thick skin that soon tanned in the strong sun of the pampas. He worked from sunrise to sunset. He was quiet, but very willing to accept any kind of work. He also worked a few hours in the village butcher shop. The butcher had taken sympathy on his Galician accent which reminded him of his own grandparents. As part of Nicanor's salary, he took home a steak that he cooked on the grill of an open fire every night when he returned to the ranch.

There was a small weekly newspaper in Trenque Lauquen, but Nicanor was never interested in reading it, only worried about his work. Nothing but work. In fact, in three years, he had saved enough money to buy a small farm. The land he bought was about 12 acres, with no electricity or housing. At the end of each working day on the farm, he worked to build a single-room hut on his new property, with walls of mud and straw that he carried in from the river in buckets. Construction was slow, but it kept him happy and satisfied as he fell into a deep sleep each night until dawn.

Six months later, he had built the four walls of the ranch and then, little by little, he assembled the roof with sheets of scrap metal that he found abandoned in the storage room of the ranch. The holes in some of them were sure to guarantee leaks, but nothing discouraged him. The finished house had a room with fireplace to boil water, and perhaps cook something very simple, and a bed with a feather mattress on a dirt floor covered with burlap bags and a latrine outside the house with walls but no roof.

Now that the house was built, there was more time for him, and he began to be interested in the girls who participated in the ritual walk around the square. Every Saturday, he would walk for hours, dressed in clean trousers, well-polished black boots, and a white shirt—the official uniform of men in search of recognition or romance with the females.

Several weeks later, he spotted a chubby, short girl with thick legs and hips; she was always walking with three or four other girls. There was nothing special about her, except for her generous breasts that seemed to explode from the dress if she breathed too deeply.

She would usually walk looking down at the ground, perhaps because of shyness or because she didn't feel comfortable with her own figure. But she never missed the Saturday walks. Her name was Josefa, he would soon learn.

Finally one Saturday, Josefa raised her eyes and exchanged glances with Nicanor, and they did the same every time they came across each other as they walked around the square. That eye contact left Nicanor very excited, happy, and with a strange sensation, like being drunk. That night he could not sleep.

—How simple life was before—

The next Saturday, he came to the plaza earlier than ever; he was very anxious to see Josefa again, but she didn't appear. When he was about to give up, he saw her in the distance, and this time, their exchange of glances was much longer, repeated on each of the laps. Sometimes there was a brief smile.

Probably five or six Saturdays passed before they dared to say a few words. Josefa pretended to have problems with her shoe and stayed behind from her friends, allowing Nicanor to come up and talk to her. He could barely get out any words, but it was enough to exchange names; enough that in future walks, there was always a smile.

She wore a different dress every weekend to get his attention. Sometimes she wore short skirts above her knees that showed her round legs, and high-heeled shoes that made her walk somewhat uncomfortably. Nicanor noticed these changes and felt an inner fire and the need to approach her and start a conversation. His strategy was to walk behind Josefa's group, and when her friends separated in different directions to go back to their homes, he followed her and got up the courage to say, "You look beautiful," with his best Galician accent. She responded with a nervous smile and, to avoid being seen by her parents, they stayed behind some trees where they were disguised by the darkness of the night.

From that day, they walked together around the square, but it took a few weeks to get up the courage to start holding hands.

—How simple life was before—

At first, their conversation was about their families, even though Nicanor had left Spain four years ago and had never heard from his family since then.

—How simple life was before—

Josefa, on the other hand, lived with her parents and two

sisters, one older and one younger than her. She had been working as a seamstress for a dressmaker ever since she finished high school. It was always busy, as it was common for people from this small town to have custom clothes made for important occasions, like baptisms, weddings, wakes, and trips to the big city.

Their first kiss was very brief, just a brushing of their lips, but a few weeks later, returning home from the square on a very hot night and protected by the darkness, the kiss was much longer. Nicanor was bold enough to touch her breasts—first above the clothes and then underneath the brassiere, to which she offered very little resistance. They were tightly embraced as if they were one body, feeling each contour, and breathing was rapid.

In the middle of this embrace, Josefa felt something strange, like an electric discharge that started at her nipples and went down to her groin. She began to tremble as if experiencing an epileptic seizure that she could not control, followed by an unusual calm. She had experienced her first orgasm at twenty-one. She didn't realize what had happened, but she liked it. After they parted, she walked home in a daze, almost without strength, and was surprised when she got into bed and found her panties wet.

During the following weeks, they would go around the square one or two times with the others, and then, trying not to be seen, they would walk away from the rest on to the dirt road and up to a thick bush on the side of the road, from which they would emerge half an hour later, adjusting themselves and their clothes and smiling from ear to ear. After several meetings in the bush like this, Nicanor came up with the idea of getting married and began the ritual process of asking Josefa's parents for her hand and arranging the preparations for the ceremony. Nicanor wanted to just go to the city hall, but her parents wanted something more formal with a church ceremony and a party to receive family and friends.

The wedding feast consisted of a delicious lamb roast drenched with red wine. At midnight, the couple took advantage of a moment of distraction, and without anyone noticing they had left the wedding party, they went by themselves to the ranch, ready to start a new life.

Josefa left her job as a seamstress in order to dedicate herself to housework, cooking, cleaning, and having children. Every day at dusk, when Nicanor returned from his work, they sat outside the ranch to drink a refreshment on the veranda that protected them from the sun or rain. They looked wordlessly out at the horizon until dinner and then finally went to sleep.

—How simple life was before—

Seven months after the wedding, they had the first child. It was said that he was born premature, but the boy weighed four kilos, so the gossiping in the town doubted that the child was premature. After the first child, Josefa was almost always pregnant. They had five more children, two boys and three girls.

All of them remained in Trenque Lauquen, except the youngest, Tomás, who was not interested in staying on the farm. He left for Buenos Aires where he got a job as an apprentice in a real estate office.

Chapter 2

Arriving in Buenos Aires, Tomás, Raúl's father, had started from the bottom and little by little worked his way up to be a partner in a real estate firm as an auctioneer of properties and farmlands. His largest clientele came from his hometown. Very soon he was able to start his own family. He married the daughter of one of the business partners and had three children of his own, Raúl and two daughters.

Don Tomás, as his colleagues called him, worked on commission. Some months, when he had many sales, he wasted money; other months, he had to borrow from family and friends.

In one of those good months, Tomás managed to get Raúl into a prestigious private primary school that concentrated on a very select group of students. There the young man met many close friends with whom he maintained lasting relationships.

The first crisis of his life was when he had to go to high school; the cost of enrolling there was twice as much as his parents could afford. Without much fanfare, he was rescued by Nicanor, his paternal grandfather, whom he barely knew because he rarely came to Buenos Aires, and when Nicanor did, he only spoke of the changes in the city since he had arrived from Spain. Thanks to the generosity of Grandfather Nicanor, Raúl was able to maintain his friendships with his classmates, who often invited him to spend the weekends at their farms or country clubs.

He began learning to play golf, and soon had a handicap of minus two, something that made him a bit of a legend amongst his friends, but especially amongst his girlfriends.

Raúl met Susana, his future wife, at a high school student dance, where only fruit juices were served and where the dancing was carefully supervised by the parents of the hostess—even as the music became louder and louder, and skirts began to shorten, and men dressed as cowboys wearing jeans.

It was not difficult to guess what attracted Raúl to Susana. Both were popular and physically attractive, which undoubtedly helped them to take the initial step; but they also shared many common interests like playing sports, the dream of traveling, and the dream of having a big family. From the day they met, there was rarely a time they were not in contact, in person or through long phone calls, in spite of her parents' and sisters' complaints.

Susana came from a very traditional family and was at teachers' college. Her father was an architect and her mother was a history teacher in a high school. They went to church together, never missing a Sunday, and never missing confession or communion.

Raúl made a very good impression on Susana's family, and soon after he graduated as a lawyer, they married, in a party many still remember. Susana and Raúl began their married life like many other couples and soon had three children.

Raúl was very fond of his children and had many phrases that he repeated often. He tried to educate them with examples. One of his favorite phrases was "Don't spit into the wind." At the time, the boys didn't understand what "spit into the wind" meant, but they soon learned on their own. Another phrase that he used often, on the spur of the moment, and sometimes without any apparent relationship to what they were discussing was: "Everything always happens for a good reason."

Fernando, the eldest son, was a law student, and it looked like he would remain a student for a very long time, even though his father hoped that one day, he would take over his law practice. The two daughters, Valeria and Maria José, were exemplary students and followed in their mother Susana's footsteps. After finishing high school, they went to University to get their diploma as high school teachers.

Raúl was confident—maybe overconfident. He knew or pretended to know everything: sports, cars, women, wines, the best restaurants, and other daily pleasures. He was always sure that when he spoke, he had a loyal audience who would listen and follow his advice. Whenever he talked about wines, he was able to recognize flavors and year of production with great accuracy. Some would say it was thanks to frequent consumption, as attested by his liver, which at the age of forty-eight had the consistency of a rock.

Raúl was very successful in his practice as a lawyer; he made a good impression on everyone. He attracted those who didn't know him with his kindness, his carefully chosen words, and his hard-to-resist smile that eased the tensions of first encounters. All this generated in his clients a confidence in his abilities, and of course, from then on, his fees had no limit. His specialty was family disputes and divorce. His best clients were women. Not only did he charge very high fees, he often ended up in bed with many of them. That was an open secret and seemed to give him even more prestige.

Raúl was six-feet tall and had an easy, wide smile. He had dark, straight hair in front with curls at the nape of the neck. Whenever he left home for any occasion, everything was always perfect. He matched the tie with the shirt, the shirt with the suit, the stockings with the shoes, and always wore the fashionable perfume according to the time of day. No one could ignore his presence—he knew it and enjoyed it.

He considered himself the best at his work, and made it known to all those around him. If something didn't go well, he always managed to blame someone else for his failure. He never acknowledged having made a mistake and never wanted to be criticized. His secretaries and colleagues learned that flattery worked well on him—and by doing so they could take advantage of benefits such as being late or taking more time for lunch.

One day, when he arrived at the office, his secretary Cristina received him, and after greeting her with a kiss on the cheek, Raúl asked, "Something new?"

"Yes. I spoke to Mrs. Ferrante. She said that she knows of you through friends who recommended you and that she wants you to look after her divorce. After talking with her for a while, I told her about your fees, and she said that they were not an obstacle. She felt very good when I told her that she had married well, but that with your help, she was going to separate even better."

Cristina arranged the first consultation at Mrs. Ferrante's house. As usual, she took care of every detail of the visit, which would help to justify Raúl's fees.

They arrived together at the mansion on the outskirts of Buenos Aires in a limousine with a driver in a black uniform and cap. After making several wrong turns through dirt roads, they finally found a wall of reddish brick about a hundred meters long with an iron gate that blocked the view from outside. The address number of Mrs. Ferrante's residence was posted on the wall.

The driver buzzed at the entry, announcing the arrival of Raúl and Cristina. They waited for the electronic door opener, and the heavy iron door opened slowly, revealing an immense mansion, looking like a replica of the Palace of Versailles at the end of a gravel road. The house was about two hundred meters from the entry gate. On both sides of the road, there were gardens with beautiful pines, carefully groomed grass and brightly colored flowerbeds.

As the limo slowly approached the mansion, Melissa Ferrante appeared at the door accompanied by two immaculately uniformed employees. The driver parked the car and opened the back door. Cristina came out first, professionally dressed in a dark gray Chanel suit with a ruffled silk blouse, followed by Raúl in a blue suit—as always made to measure by an Italian tailor—and a white shirt with French cuffs, cufflinks, and his initials embroidered on the cuff.

They introduced themselves and entered the mansion where Mrs. Ferrante led them to the library, a room that inspired reading and that was perfect for this occasion. There was a large table in the center of the room with twenty chairs, but they opted for three armchairs in a corner of the immense room lined with shelves full of leather-covered books.

Melissa Ferrante was fifty-four years old, with a flat expression and no makeup. She was dressed in a black, shapeless outfit that further revealed her lack of attention to her looks. With such an appearance, it was hard to imagine that there was anything that could excite her or could make her smile or cry. Despite her depressed image, the meeting seemed to go well. Cristina opened her portfolio and took out a pad of paper to take notes. Raúl gave a brief introduction about the areas that were going to be discussed. He needed to know the status of the relationship with her husband.

"Look, Raúl, can I call you by your name?"

"Of course," said Raúl.

Melissa had a little difficulty trying to explain her situation, but after a few minutes, thanks to Raúl's friendly smiles, she was seemed to manage.

"During the last ten years, we have lost all intimacy. He says to me all the time, 'You are frigid,' whether we are alone or in the company of friends. It makes me feel very embarrassed every time. He degrades me in the presence of friends and sometimes even strangers."

She continued to say that her husband was relentless with his constant verbal aggressions. He rarely shared anything with her and made her ask for money for her own personal expenses.

"Many nights he doesn't come home, and he never has an explanation."

"I'm a little surprised he didn't ask you for a divorce." Raúl said, adding, "Though I suspect he knows that getting a divorce will cost him a fortune."

"My life is very empty, Raúl, and I don't want to continue living this way. It has taken away everything: dignity, friends, independence."

"Don't worry," Raúl said. "We will help you in everything that is necessary."

They explained to Melissa that afternoon that they were going to investigate and document the husband's escapades.

"The firm has a team of private investigators who will follow him day and night. We will identify all his assets, including accounts abroad, properties, and investments in the bond and stock market."

They also planned to contact witnesses who would testify to his verbal abuse toward her. Melissa signed papers, authorizing them to make all these inquiries, approving the basic hourly fees plus a percentage of the total she would receive in the settlement. She signed almost without reading, and this time the one who smiled was Raúl.

"How long is the whole process going to take?" Melissa asked.

Raúl explained that they would meet twice more before sending all the documentation to the court. He commented that this was common practice, although sometimes more data might be needed and there could be delays. He estimated that in two months, everything could be completed.

Before they left, Melissa said, "Raúl, I have no interest in the house in Punta del Este. I prefer this house and the apartment in Récoleta."

"We'll talk about that, but I don't foresee that there should be any difficulty."

Outside, the limo driver was waiting for them, taking them back to the office where Raúl and Cristina prepared the work plan. The next day, they would call the potential witnesses and contact the investigators to follow Mr. Ferrante. They would investigate all their bank accounts and identify the properties he owned.

It was not difficult to follow Mr. Ferrante because he didn't take any precautions to avoid being seen entering the hotels around the Pan-American Highway with a different glamorous blonde on each occasion. In addition, there were plenty of witnesses who were happy to be able to help Melissa. All of them corroborated the verbal abuse that she had received. The financial investigations demanded more time than expected, because in addition to the properties, he had bank accounts in Switzerland and other tax havens.

When they finally completed all the documentation, they invited Mrs. Ferrante to the office. This was a ploy to impress the client, since the offices were on the top floor of a luxurious tower overlooking the Rio de la Plata. From the enormous windows you could admire the silvery surface of the river, light reflecting everywhere on a sunny day with the sailboats rocking in its waters. The office walls were covered with original paintings by famous Argentine artists, such as Fader and Castagnino.

Melissa arrived promptly, and Raúl and Cristina immediately noticed a change in her appearance compared to the previous meeting. She smiled effortlessly, wore a brightly colored dress, and had undoubtedly spent a lot of time at the hairdresser. She displayed a modern haircut and a fresh manicure.

Raúl and Cristina laid the documentation they had collected on the table, including photos of the husband entering the hotels, always accompanied by a different blonde. They included the names of the witnesses who would participate in her defense and told her about the support offered by her old friends. Also, for the first time, she became aware of all the assets her husband owned.

"Raúl, I think I'm going to be a very attractive divorcée, especially because of the size of his bank account."

Raúl reassured her that the husband's lawyers would not be able to disprove all this evidence and that they should be willing to negotiate. Raúl always showed signs of being very confident of a favorable final verdict, something endearing to the ears of his clients. Melissa left the office happy and impressed with the professionalism of Raúl and his team. She was very close to breaking free.

. . .

The next meeting would be between her and Raúl for him to train her on how to behave in court and how to answer the questions that her husband's lawyers would be expected to ask her.

Raúl had warned her that, although everything was very clear, it was common for lawyers to set up a trap, and they should be prepared.

"In these ten years, Melissa, have you had any adventures that might come up in the trial?" Raúl asked.

"Raúl, I guarantee you that in the last ten years, I have not had any contact with man or woman."

As was his routine, Raúl arranged this meeting to be at the Sheraton Hotel restaurant, where he had lunch with the client in a private space separated from the rest of the dining room. The manager and the waiters knew him and appreciated his visits and the generous tips he left. The Melissa that showed up that day was wearing a provocative dress, lots of makeup, and a broad smile. It seemed her style had completely changed during the process of the divorce.

They ordered lunch, and Raúl was surprised when she ordered a Campari with the appetizer and chardonnay with the main course. She asked for salmon with hazelnut sauce, and he ordered filet mignon, medium rare.

It didn't take long for Raúl to explain to Melissa all the obstacles that might arise during the trial, and he also promised that he and his team would support her in whatever was necessary. Melissa was an intelligent woman and quickly grasped the whole situation.

After finishing the exquisite lunch and drinking a liquor with coffee, they stood up very close to each other and melted into a long hug and a kiss. As in so many other times in the past, Raúl wasted no time calling the manager to arrange a room in the hotel, where they would arrive separately.

Melissa went to the room first, and by the time Raúl arrived, she was barely dressed. Despite her ten years of abstinence, sex was apparently like riding a bicycle, something that was not forgotten. It helped that the alcohol they had at lunch loosened any inhibition. They were at it for about four hours, first one on top, then the other, until they had barely enough energy left to say goodbye with a kiss. The next time they would see each other, it would be in court.

· · ·

Melissa dressed, arranging her hair and makeup as well as she could, and left the hotel without any thoughts of where she would go. She was confused and a little sore and walked with some discomfort. But inside she felt like a woman again. It was a feeling that only a woman who had been ignored for so long could understand; she had been reborn, proud because she was again an alive human being.

Yes, I am a woman, she thought, looking around with an air of confidence. "Thanks, Raúl," she said to herself. "Thank you for helping me to be reborn as a woman."

Regaining her confidence as a woman was, perhaps, more important to her than winning a divorce judgment against her husband. She knew that what she had done was not right, because she and Raúl were still married. But more than the infidelity, this was something therapeutic for her. To justify her actions, she said to herself that some psychiatrists even used sex with their patients as a treatment.

. . .

Raúl had only been thinking about his fees, and taking Melissa to bed was a special benefit of his job. He had no remorse, only a little worry about the fact that if Susana learned of the affair, it would cost him a lot of money!

There was nothing in their separation demands that they didn't get it: the apartment in Recoleta, the mansion in Castelar, half of everything in the bank accounts and monthly compensation for life. Melissa had changed in a single day into an attractive millionaire full of life and hope, thanks to Raúl.

Raúl never got tired of hearing, "Thanks, Raúl! Thanks, Raúl! You are the best lawyer!"

And he repeated to himself, "I *am* the best lawyer."

Chapter 3

Raúl was once again the center of attention in his family. He was a brilliant lawyer, as his mother would say. In every occasion they got together in the past, everyone expected his touch of flair. This particular reunion had been organized in an old house that had once belonged to one of the richest families in Buenos Aires. The new owners rented it for special events, and this reunion was indeed very special.

It was a typical spring day in Buenos Aires with the sun peeking out of the clouds, but not enough to raise the temperature. The locals complained as usual about the cold and the humidity.

The stately mansion was in a corner of the fancy neighborhood of Belgrano, surrounded by embassies and other grand mansions. It had two floors, with the exterior in cream-colored plaster and partly covered with ivy. The entrance hall was large and luxurious, with walls covered with white marble and the tile floors with alternating black and white marble pieces.

When entering, there was soft music playing. It was easy to recognize Enya and some other popular classics. In a room at the back of the house was Raúl's coffin. It seemed like an ordinary day; Raúl was wearing his best clothes. Always well-groomed with a white shirt and blue suit. Now, he lacked only the smile. His death, Cristina recounted, had occurred in the office, after a fight with a customer who had come knocking on the door in a fury.

Cristina remembered waiting a few minutes before entering, but came in when Raúl didn't respond to her call. He was lying on the ground, unconscious. She began shouting hysterically, which attracted the attention of the other lawyers and secretaries who were in the office. One of them confirmed that Raúl didn't have a pulse and called an ambulance, but it was too late—he had suffered a fatal heart attack.

His colleagues had the unpleasant task of reporting the bad news to family and friends. For many, his death was very difficult to accept, particularly for his mother, children, and sisters. Susana's reaction was guarded; maybe it would hit her sometime later.

The visitation in the old house was very busy because Raúl had always been popular—judges, colleagues, polo players, a former justice minister, and many elegant women splashed with attractive perfumes.

"Hello, Juan Carlos, how are you doing? I have not seen you for a while" Ramiro said. Juan Carlos and Ramiro were distant relatives.

"I didn't know you knew Raúl."

"Look, no one knows Raúl better than me. Our , friendship goes back to high school, and from the first day we met, it was clear we had something in common, almost closer than brothers. Afterward, we were classmates at University as law students. We shared so many things, so many adventures. The good and the bad. But always together."

Sometimes the conversations were interrupted by young ladies dressed in black uniforms with white shirts and bow ties around their necks, offering drinks and delicious snacks.

In another corner of the house, there was a group of women, who, from their comments, didn't seem to be very good friends with Susana. In one of the reception rooms, away from the others, was the former Mrs. Ferrante, who no longer had the bitter face of her first interview with Raúl. She was smiling, accompanied by a gentleman a little younger than herself, and both wore a Caribbean tan.

"Hello, dear," Melissa said, addressing Cristina. "I want to introduce you to my partner, Guillermo. I always talk to him about you and Raúl, about everything you did for me, not only in the professional aspect, because you are undoubtedly the best, but because you took me out of a spiritual depression and helped me to live again like a normal person."

The conversation between them continued.

There were also some Trenque Lauquen cousins whom Raúl detested because they reminded him of his humble origins. None of them was dressed appropriately for the elegance of this gathering. There was no denying that they were peasants—they laughed loudly, and every time they were offered food, they emptied the serving tray.

In another corner of the room there was a group of people who seemed to be having a great time as the laughing could be heard from all around. No surprise, in the center of the group was Chacho Ramírez, an old friend of the family who always told stories of all kinds, innocent or spicy, according to each group and occasion. Someone had the bad taste to ask him if he had any new jokes. It was just what El Chacho needed to start an unending series of stories.

"Listen to this one. I heard it recently. It's about an old man who had a small pond in his farm, and after a long time, he decided to go check if everything was in order. He took a basket to take advantage of the walk and bring wild fruits, blackberries, raspberries, and some apples found along the way. As he approached the lagoon, he heard animated voices and laughter that came from a group of women who were bathing completely naked. Upon seeing him, the women panicked and swam into the deepest part of the pond, leaving only their heads out of the water.

"One of them shouted: *'We will not get out of the water until you leave.' The old man replied, 'I didn't come here to see you swim or leave the lake naked.' Lifting the basket, he told them, 'I've come to feed the crocodile.'"*

Everyone imagined the women leaving the pond in a panic, not worrying about their nakedness. Soon, everybody in his audience was laughing.

Chacho was one of the poker club members who met every Thursday just for the excuse of playing cards, but especially to try a new Scotch whiskey each week and always with a happy ending.

Although Raúl wanted to win at everything, in poker games he was often the loser, although it didn't bother him much as he had fun sharing time with his best friends, and they only played for nickels and dimes. Raúl always lost playing poker because his friends had figured out that if he didn't have a good hand, he would always scratch his head, while if he had good cards, he would rub on his earlobe. It was almost like showing the cards. That's why he was such a frequent loser.

Raúl was born in Buenos Aires and, as a typical "Porteño," he often bragged about his accomplishments, like owning the best car, or the successes of his children, or his trips to exotic places. Even so, everyone agreed that he was a good and faithful friend and willing to help anyone who needed it.

Everyone noted that Susana and Raúl had been married for twenty-four years and lamented that they were not going to celebrate with them the party they were planning for their silver wedding anniversary.

Father Iturrieta, the director of the San Javier School that the Franciscan priests had built next to the convent, could not be expected to miss a reunion such as this. Raúl and several of his friends had gone to San Javier, a school of moderate standards but with high-class aspirations. Father Iturrieta was very strict and that discipline was what attracted families who wanted a good religious education for their children. The boys and girls of the San Javier school wore uniforms that distinguished them from those who attended public school, who could wear whatever they wanted and made fun of those who had to wear the same clothing every day.

On Sundays, Father Iturrieta's long sermons were an excruciating experience. He had some favorite readings like "The Prodigal Son," but at the end of the sermon, he usually managed to tell the congregation that they were all "bad people"—because they were late for mass or class, or because they didn't wear ties, or because they didn't shine their shoes. He got especially angry with those girls who wore their skirts above their knees and reprimanded the boys if he caught them touching the breasts of big Josefina, even though she let them do it and liked it. He would give grief if they confessed that they had masturbated. His sermons were a masochistic invitation to return the following Sunday that no one could escape—the priest took attendance, and anyone missing would be given a surprise test on Monday about what he had preached in the sermon. Not only did you have to be present, but you had to pay attention.

. . .

At a funeral, there was always someone interested in what happened to life after death. It was easy enough to understand that the body itself disappeared. Many had seen the decomposition of the remains of a deceased relative. But what the worms could not break down was the spirit, the ideas and thoughts of that individual. People wondered what happened to that intangible matter floating in the air after dying. Of course, there were scientific explanations, religious and popular legends, all unconfirmed, how one moved on to the next life.

Since they could not talk about women, cars, or sports with the priest, and because Easter was near, the attendees began to talk with Father Iturrieta about the resurrection.

"What was the resurrection?"

Father Iturrieta was surrounded either by those who wanted to score points with him or who didn't know anyone else in the visitation crowd. The soft, yellowish light of the room gave them all a sickly color, even though Iturrieta, like a good Basque, had a square head and permanently rosy cheeks. They talked about the beliefs of different religions about what happened after death. Some spoke of reincarnation; but the priest, even though he himself was about eighty-five years old, didn't accept any alternative to the doctrine and was upset when he heard that one of the students of the San Javier School had converted to Buddhism.

The priest insisted on the teachings of the Bible—that is, after death, the spirit is separated from the body; and if judged to be sinful, sent to hell or purgatory; and if judged to be free of sin, to heaven, waiting to be resurrected after Judgment Day.

One of the people participating in the discussion, a marketing director of an insurance company, told Father Iturrieta, "Do you know, Father, what the problem is with the Catholic Church? They have no idea what good 'marketing' is. They don't promise you anything, and if one doesn't meet all the demands, they send you to hell."

He continued. "Muslims have the best plan. They tell their followers that life on earth serves to prepare for a better life after death. For that reason, they have no problem becoming martyrs by committing suicide with explosives wrapped around their bodies."

The priest insisted that after death, the spirit separates from the body until the day of final judgment. In his softest voice, he replied, "Religion is not a business. It is something deeper and spiritual. Christ didn't die on the cross to drive an industry."

But that was not enough to convince the marketing director. "Father, you know that in the next twenty years, the world population of Muslims will easily match the number of Christians."

It seemed that Father Iturrieta didn't listen to him or pay attention to him. The conversation continued. Vicente was part of the group that was arguing with Father Iturrieta. Vicente was an owner of a grocery store, fat, with a prominent abdomen, a day-old beard, and ruddy cheeks. Raúl had helped him win a trial against the owners of the building where he had his business and for that reason, he idolized Raúl and, even though it was obvious that he was not at the same social level of the rest of the group, he was not too timid to speak his mind.

"Look, Father, I don't think there is life after death, so for now, I'm going to enjoy all the pleasures of life, eat well, drink the best wines, smoke cigars, go out with prostitutes, because nobody knows what comes next."

This caused a few smiles, of course, which they tried to hide from the priest's sight.

Gustavo was the student who had converted to Buddhism. He had always been different, "freaky," according to some, with an almost dirty appearance, long hair, disheveled and tangled like a nest of sparrow. But he was very peaceful and friendly, never got into fights, and hung out with others who were similarly peaceful. By the end of high school, he had collected some money doing odd jobs in the neighborhood and ended up traveling to Thailand for six months, where it didn't take him long to be absorbed into Buddhism. His pacifism and openness to new ideas were a perfect combination. He began to frequent the Temples and to get together with priests or monks dressed in orange blankets and shaved heads, with whom he had long conversations. According to him, converting to Buddhism didn't require any ceremony, simply sharing ideas and spreading them.

That day at the wake, Gustavo revealed his beliefs to friends and explained that Raúl's spirit would soon enter the cycle of death, followed by reincarnation in the body of some stranger.

. . .

Later, Raúl's remains were taken to a vault in the Recoleta. That, for all, was the end of someone who had lived his life intensely with his family and friends, and in his work.

It was time now for the family to be together and share memories and sorrows. Tears and smiles.

Chapter 4

After the funeral, Raúl's daughters questioned their mother about the idea of reincarnation.

"What Gustavo said left us thinking," Valeria asked. "Did he mean that Dad's spirit is going to get into someone else?"

Susana responded with some annoyance, since it was something they should already have learned after so many years at Catholic school.

"Although many religions believe they know what happens after death, no one really knows the truth. It is a mystery, although the Catholic Church believes in the resurrection"

She continued. "As Catholics we follow the Holy Scriptures, which maintain that at the moment of death, the spirit separates from the body and is judged by God. Those who have followed the teachings of Christ go to heaven, reserved for the saints; most people who only have minor sins will be sent to purgatory to be cleansed, and at the end of the world, there will be a resurrection of all bodies on the day of final judgment, and our bodies will meet again with our spirits. Except those who went to hell. That is why, when someone dies, it is said that they 'go on to a better life.'

"According to Gustavo and his interpretation of Buddhism, life doesn't end when the body dies. I know that Buddhism speaks of a new life after death. This belief is accepted by many, but nobody has proof that this is the only truth."

Valeria shook her head and said, "It scares me to think that I could be talking to a person, and inside, there is another who listens to everything."

"Did you ever think that you were with someone who had been reincarnated by an acquaintance of yours?" Susana asked.

"Yes, I often have a sense of déjà vu. Maybe it happens when I meet someone who I used to know in a previous life. Thinking about this is scary."

Maria José added, "I want to choose who I get to be reincarnated into. I don't want to end up inside some random stranger or a weirdo."

Gustavo had explained that everything depended on one's actions, and if a person was good, he would be rewarded with good karma, someone who would make him happy. If it were true, we would never have problems. It was a very idealistic thought.

Maria José explained to her mother what Gustavo had told them. "Buddhists consider death as a temporary separation from the materialistic world. The new spirit learns from previous experiences, and thus, with each reincarnation, the spirit becomes a more evolved version than the previous one.

The Buddhist teachings maintain that, when dying, the body was separated from the spirit, and the soul and ideas of the deceased were passed on to the reincarnated entity, which was like a shell for this new bubble. Gustavo called this the 'pécora,' combining the thoughts and feelings of the deceased. The pécora that moved to the reincarnated included the thoughts, mind, ideas, intellect, spirit, soul, character, and personality of the deceased. This would, of course, have a significant impact on the life of the reincarnated. Gustavo explained that the person who was reincarnated was called the "cascara" . The newly reincarnated was a mixture of both—the previous body carried the mind and soul, which now mixed with the mind and soul of the deceased.

Valeria had asked Gustavo, "How long does it take the pécora to reincarnate in a new person?"

Gustavo had explained that the time established to reincarnate in another body was forty-nine days, although other Buddhist currents believed that the spirit could wait up to six months before entering a new body.

Maria José had said, "We will recognize our father?"

"Only if you can identify some words or gestures that were typical of him. But he cannot tell you anything."

When the new host received the pécora, Gustavo had explained, the new person immediately became a combination of both, and in each reincarnated, the contribution to the new person was not necessarily the best part of each. In other words, the reincarnated was not a mirror of one of the two; it had a new personality, and the pécora did not retain all the previous characteristics.

Gustavo insisted, "With each reincarnation, the new individual becomes better than the previous versions." But this was not necessarily true sometimes it was worse.

To convince his friends of the idea of reincarnation, Gustavo used stories that were in the public domain but had never been scientifically confirmed. One of the best stories was that of Ruth Simmons, who in 1952 was treated with regressive hypnosis to allow her to recall experiences since birth. After waking from one of those sessions, she began to speak with a strong Irish accent and to remember details of her life in the nineteenth century, when she was Bridey Murphy and lived in Belfast. Much of what this woman mentioned could not be proven, but she remembered the names of two people from whom she bought her groceries, who were later identified in the city records. This story was documented in the movie *Finding Bridey Murphy*.

Gustavo argued that the reincarnates should follow very strict rules. They had confidential information and were not allowed to say that they were reincarnated, although they could provide information indirectly through gestures or phrases that they previously used and that identified them during their own lives.

The reincarnated knew that if they announced their identity directly to their family or friends or if they suffered an abnormal death such as suicide, the pécora exploded immediately like a soap bubble and disappeared forever.

It was the end of their cycle of reincarnation. This cycle continued indefinitely, and that was why, perhaps, multiple reincarnations explained why we were so different from each other by carrying within our small bodies a multitude of individuals.

The daily activities of the reincarnated were not very different from the rest of the people, and that was why they can't be identified. Yet, they developed an intense need to see their children, their family and friends, and would try to be recognized. They knew that, if they announced who they were, it was the end for them.

Gustavo asked the crowd, "How many times have you met someone who by their language, phrases or gestures reminds you of someone you have met before?"

Raúl's daughters had listened carefully, but their main interest was to know if one day they might see or recognize their father in a stranger because of his manners or his words. It didn't surprise them to hear people say, "I know a neighbor that reminds me of my grandfather," and other things like that.

It was also common to hear stories about people who suddenly showed drastic changes in their personality. For example, someone who used to be shy and introverted became bold and determined, or someone messy started to be efficient and organized, or one who once was humble became a braggart.

Gustavo explained, "From the time we are born, little by little, we find the path to where we are going, but it is difficult to know what happens in the end. We know that we can't escape death, but what most torments us is the mystery of not knowing the final destination. For Buddhism and many other religions, the final destination is reincarnation.

. . .

Meanwhile, Raúl's pécora was still wandering, trying to find a perfect place. Raúl thought, *My shell should be someone who is prepared to be the best; I will guide him to be successful in business and also in relationships with women.*

The spirit of Raúl, still searching, knew it would be difficult to find another Raúl better than the one who had just passed away. Finding someone compatible with all his needs was going to be hard—and even harder to change someone who already might have a distinctive personality.

For him, it would be easier to look for someone young without very well-differentiated characteristics; neutral, but with the potential to fulfill all his aspirations. His first candidate was a boy of twenty-three from an influential and powerful family. He had six brothers, and he was the second youngest, very handsome, and had never been interested in family business. He was mostly interested in the arts. He had studied at the Faculty of Fine Arts and wanted to be a painter. He was interested in neo-impressionism and sculpture. He had been to many exhibits in many museums, but his strongest experience was when he first visited some of the museums in Europe. At twenty-three, he had shown no interest in women, even though he had plenty of friends.

Raúl followed him for a while, but he knew that artists as a group were always "starving," and he worried about the young man's disinterest in business and women, and his focus on humble lifestyle.

A few weeks later, Raúl found another candidate. He was young and was studying engineering. His appearance was average at best, nothing great, but mentally, he was very conservative. To him, all the women studying engineering were more interested in numbers than in any relationships. They were not very attractive to him. This man certainly didn't match the guy Raúl had in mind.

Raúl continued his search because it was very important to choose the right person, since he was going to live with him for the rest of his life. He had a maximum of six months to make the decision.

Raúl knew he had to choose well and was in no hurry, because if the new host had a personality opposite of his pécora, it would cause constant conflict.

Those in whom the pécora was dominant and the host could accept the new personality would have a more stable life. In these cases, the compatibility increased its potential, either negative or positive, and in the reincarnated its original virtues could be drastically modified or its qualities or defects changed to other characteristics that had not previously.

With that knowledge, Raúl was still hoping to find the ideal candidate.

Raúl's search for his shell continued. He had begun to consider a young man of only seventeen years of age, thinking that someone that age could transform him in his own way. Perhaps what attracted Raúl the most were the young man's natural aptitudes and possible potential to continue with all Raúl's dreams.

Chapter 5

Almost at the same time that Raúl's funeral was going on, a more dramatic situation was taking place in the outskirts of the city. Norberto, a young union leader, had been kidnapped a few days earlier, and his body had just been found, riddled with bullets. No one knew why, but there was a great deal of speculation.

Norberto had gone to buy cigarettes at the newsstand on the corner, just a block from his home, in the neighborhood where he was born. It was ten in the morning on a sunny day. Everyone knew Norberto. Some feared him, and some at least disliked him because of his intimidating character, but no one would have wished him death, much less a violent death.

According to the witnesses, a car suddenly appeared out of nowhere, pulled up next to Norberto, and before he could react to defend himself, two masked men got out and threw him into the back seat of the car, which then took off like a bullet.

The neighbors only managed to recognize a blue Japanese car, but they all told different stories to the police, and no one was sure of the number of the license plate.

This neighborhood where Norberto had grown up, "La Matanza," was a neighborhood of modest low houses. Some of them had a small garden in the front, and many of them had been renovated to add another bedroom for a son or daughter who married and stayed to live with the parents, even when they had children of their own.

—*How simple life was then.*—

Norberto lived with his parents in an area where there were many factories with tall chimneys blowing dirty black smoke. Those factories gave work to thousands of people. Most of them lived in homes that they had built when they left the farms to work in the big city in search of better wages.

La Matanza had many cattle slaughterhouses that provided the meat to feed not only the city, but also enough to export to neighboring countries. Animals arrived every day, in dirty trucks covered with droppings, and the smell and squeals of the animals, who seemed to know what was in store for them, made life intolerable for anyone who had not been born in that neighborhood and grown accustomed to it long ago.

For three days, no one knew of the whereabouts of Norberto. It was as if the earth had swallowed him. His family received two phone calls for ransom, but they turned out to be hoaxes from those who wanted to take advantage of the situation and were soon found to have no relationship at all with the captors. Norberto's family was desperate; the police had no news or clues. Everyone expected the worst.

The car was never found. The family organized their own search. They hired a private investigator—a retired police officer who was known to the family.

A week after the kidnapping, a fisherman saw a body on the side of the river 200 kilometers from Buenos Aires and reported it to the local police. It took two days to confirm without a doubt that it was the body of Norberto.

The funeral had been organized in a local funeral home in the neighborhood of La Matanza that had room for two funerals at a time; they needed a big place because they expected many visitors. Norberto was known by everybody.

As in so many funerals, the local parish priest assisted the family members in their misery even though, as one might imagine, they had not been very frequent supporters of the church. Norberto's parents never imagined that their son could die like that—murdered and unable to defend himself. They considered Norberto immortal, invincible. They were devastated and looked for comfort from the rest of the family and friends.

At the funeral, everyone spoke of his career with admiration. As is customary on such occasions, his successes were exalted, and no one mentioned his bad temper or his reputation as a bully. His protector was there, a man with whom he had developed a relationship, almost like father and son. He had encouraged Norberto to enter the union. He, too, felt as if he had lost a son. He recalled that despite not having any work experience, Norberto had managed to join the union of the sheet metal workers, one of the most powerful unions in the country, and had risen rapidly in the ranks, to be secretary of the union president. No one spoke to the president without Norberto's permission.

Everyone got a laugh out of recalling Norberto's manner of speaking. He rarely spoke in a normal voice. For him, it was always shouting hoarsely, as if those who listened to him were deaf or far away, and his speech was always decorated with cursing.

Norberto would often say to his opponents, always with an air of superiority, "We're not on the same level, you know."

When Norberto finished high school, he followed the example of many members of his family. He became the bodyguard of a mobster: one who had several different businesses, including loaning money with very high interest rates and dealing in illegal drugs. Norberto made sure that those who had a loan would pay without delay. Everyone was afraid of having a visit from him.

Even by high school, and in spite of his small size, he was showing the typical bully behavior and intimidating half the students in the school, while the other half had almost servile admiration of his power. It was known that he owned an eight-inch switchblade—he showed it whenever he wanted to scare someone—in addition to the gun that his father had given him at age eighteen as a gift for his high school graduation. He was a bully with the girls, too, and many of them surrendered to his sexual advances for fear of being the subject of gossip throughout the school. He had no respect for anyone who didn't follow his rules.

When he went out for a walk in the neighborhood, he was always in the company of three or four of his cronies, who were ready to react if anyone dared to provoke him.

As the mobster's bodyguard, Norberto make a lot of money. As soon as he could, he bought a luxurious car and wore expensive, fancy clothes. He was always seen in a suit with a black shirt and a gray tie. Almost a mobster uniform. He constantly had a lit cigarette hanging from the side of his mouth. He smoked only expensive American cigarettes.

Norberto was married to Norma, a girl with a perfectly sculpted body. She had worked the streets to escape the slums, until she met Norberto, and then everything changed for her. Shortly after getting married, she wanted to move to an apartment far from La Matanza where all his family had lived all their lives. Despite his complaints, they bought an apartment in the Flores neighborhood, knowing he was only going to be there to sleep. The rest of the day, he would be in his office, at the union, in La Matanza at his parents' house, or drinking beer with his friends.

Norberto and Norma had two small children. They bought them the newest and most expensive toys, perhaps as a response to the shortage of their own childhoods. Away from the house, Norberto was to everybody *"the macho man,"* but at home things were different. Norma totally dominated him, and he had to fulfill all her wishes.

Norma was naturally lazy; she never cleaned the house, cooked, or cared for the kids. Her only sport was to go to the beauty salon and to go shopping, and if Norberto didn't give her enough money, she would start a fight, insulting him and threatening to not let him enter the house.

Norma didn't get along with Norberto's family. It was suspected that she had married him to escape her past, and for that reason, no one was surprised when she arrived late to the funeral, accompanied by some friends who looked more like they were going to a party than to the funeral of their friend's husband.

Like the newspapers, most of those at the funeral were discussing the possible motives for the crime and who could have committed it, especially trying to explain the violence with which they had killed him. Many rumors circulated. Norberto was the right hand of the union president and was in charge of paying the social agencies. It was known that when the medical centers taking care of the union members asked for a payment in advance, this implied a juicy bribe for Norberto. It was also known that other workers competed for his position. Also during his time working for the mobster, he had been able to supply some of his own customers with drugs. It could be that they had killed him for revenge, for an unpaid account, or to rob him, since he always carried a lot of money in his wallet.

Norberto had two brothers who were very close to him. They had never accepted Norma. They were at the funeral surrounded by friends from the neighborhood, and the older brother said, "I am sure this whore had him killed. Everyone loved our brother. He always helped everybody." Those gathered around him nodded to confirm his words.

One of these friends told him, "Look, I didn't want to tell you, but the other day, I saw Norma. She was on the street in a fancy neighborhood looking for clients, just like the old days."

Norberto had taken her off the streets, but she had never thanked him. In fact, being a prostitute was still her profession; she had never really given it up. He must have known that nobody in her profession ever really gave it up.

What nobody knew was that a few months before his death, knowing the risk of his work, Norberto and Norma had taken out insurance on his life for a million pesos, and she was the only beneficiary of that policy. It was as if Norberto's signature on that insurance was a signature on his death warrant. Norma and Norberto had a relationship full of constant fights, and they didn't try to hide it. They fought as much in front of friends and family as they did when they were alone.

Norberto was born a bully like his father. The violence was in his genes, and he had a natural talent to protect his covert businesses. Nobody had challenged his ethics, and asking for bribes was natural to him. His arrogance had brought him many enemies, but he ignored all those who didn't agree with him, and as he always ended up telling them, "We're not on the same level, you know."

Norberto's body was not on display. He was in the funeral home with a closed casket due to the condition of the body found seven days after his death. A nauseating smell didn't go unnoticed, barely concealed by the perfume of the flower wreaths that filled the place. There were uniformed police officers, in case the killer showed up, and also other police in civilian clothes, posing as family or friends while searching for information.

Norma stayed at the funeral home surrounded only by her girlfriends. They spoke almost in secret and didn't talk to Norberto's parents. Everyone commented that she seemed not to shed a tear. Surely, she wouldn't want to ruin her makeup. Despite the cold night, many of the guests were outdoors smoking or drinking coffee and scotch with the excuse of warming up.

No one went to sleep that night. It was a night of stories and memories. Someone said that, as a boy, Norberto and his neighborhood friends played games, and one of those games was to take the train without a ticket and see who could travel more station stops without being caught. The trick was to climb into the middle of the train; there were always two guards who approached from each end of the train to the center, checking that all passengers had a ticket. If they found someone without a ticket, they would pull their ears and give them a good kick in the ass that was remembered for days. Back then, nobody criticized the guards for that kind of discipline.

—*How simple life was then.*—

Norberto's teammates from the neighborhood soccer team were also at the funeral. One jokingly said that although Norberto was not a very skillful player, he made the team because he was the only one who ever brought the soccer balls.

After that long night of laughter, stories, and many drinks, the director funeral home called for the family to come and say goodbye and to touch the coffin one last time. The parents could not stop crying. They hugged friends and relatives and asked why he deserved such a punishment.

The coffin was carried in a black car with windows on the side, which allowed a view the coffin. Family and friends followed in a long procession of cars to the cemetery where the priest gave the last rites before the cremation. A curtain separated the family from the casket which held Norberto's body, and then, as they were all leaving the place, the cremation began. They smelled the burning wood from the cremation, and one of the friends who had been drinking too much said, "Hey, guys, you better hurry because I smell a barbecue, and I don't want to miss it!"

. . .

In the days and weeks after the funeral, Norberto's family tried to reorganize their life, but to no surprise, Norma never went back to see her in-laws. Even now, she really had no interest in being a mother and had left her children to be taken care of by her parents. Soon afterward, she moved into a three-bedroom apartment in the downtown area that she bought with the insurance money from the policy she had taken on Norberto. This brought all kinds of suspicion upon her. Nothing was ever proven, and she went on with her career, although she didn't need to go back to the streets like in the old days. This time, she put up ads in the newspapers with a menu of services she offered as a luxury prostitute. The apartment was soon filled with high-class clients. She had so much work that soon she was able to employ two more girls to work for her. Norma eventually became the most popular Madam in the city.

Chapter 6

After wandering aimlessly, Raúl's pécora finally entered the shell of Alfredo, a young man of eighteen years.

Alfredito, as his friends called him, was the son of the owners of a typical neighborhood store, behind which was the family home at the back of the building. The store, like so many others, was the place where the neighbors did their shopping before supermarkets appeared. The store was on the corner of a busy central block, and the owners knew all the customers by name and often sold to them on credit, based on the trust that the majority would pay at the end of the month when they received their monthly salary payments.

Alfredito was very shy, quiet, unsure of himself. He never looked into anyone's eyes or started a conversation. He went to high school, but he wasn't the least bit interested; he didn't really care if he graduated. His future was in his parents' store.

He played football on the neighborhood team with his many friends, where they competed with other nearby teams. At soccer, he was very skilled, but when his parents needed help in the store, that came first, and he would not play. He didn't dare to talk to girls of his age, even though there were one or two in the neighborhood that he liked. He was of medium height, thin, and with blond hair, without any physical characteristic that made him remarkable, except for the typical teenage acne, which made him even more timid.

After being penetrated by Raúl's pécora, the changes were gradual, and even though Alfredito tried to resist this, Raúl's typical bold behavior made the young man nervous because he didn't know how to control it.

After being penetrated by Raúl, the pécora took a dominant role. Raul always gave his opinions, and Alfredo had to listen to him. The young man didn't understand what was happening to him, and he was constantly afraid to face the day, not knowing how he would react. This caused him great anxiety, but little by little, he adapted.

One afternoon, while attending the store alone, Doña Luisa arrived. She was one of the regular customers of the store. She was about fifty years old, her hair dyed bottle-blond. She was plump and provocative with clothes too small to contain all that body; skirt above the knees, too much make-up, and big breasts proudly displayed with a cleavage so deep it left very little to the imagination. Those breasts always tormented Alfredo when she deliberately and provocatively showed them off in front of his eyes.

On this occasion, after she paid her bill and knowing no one could see him, Alfredo was encouraged and, without really being conscious of his words, he said, "Doña Luisa, you have such beautiful breasts. Do you think I could touch them?"

"What did you say?!" Doña Luisa replied in a high tone, feigning anger.

Alfredito quickly retreated and pretended that he has said something different.

"We have some fresh pies. Would you like to try them?"

She left the store, thinking to herself, *you finally woke up. I would gladly let you touch them.*

An hour later Alfredo was still shaking until he finally recovered and was surprised when she returned that afternoon, smiling and in a very friendly mood. With a sweet tone of voice, she said, "Alfredito, I came back because I kept thinking about the pies you recommended, and I wanted to try them."

Before Alfredo could say anything, she added, "Maybe you'd like to try?" —while pointing at her breasts with a mischievous look in her eye.

After that, everyone noticed a profound change in Alfredo. His parents didn't know how to react when he started making changes to the store, including a section of ready-to-go meals and fancier specialty items which were unusual for a neighborhood store. Surprisingly, the business began to attract new customers, and the store needed to be enlarged to take over part of their house. Because of this success, other stores in the area began to lose customers.

After a while, Alfredo became accustomed to his new personality and even began to enjoy it. All his anxieties from the beginning had dissipated, but he never forgot what he had learned in the neighborhood of his childhood, and he always used those experiences in his dialogues with Raúl the pécora.

His friends and family saw a positive change in Alfredo. He began to smile and made customers feel welcome. He became more independent and started saving some money to buy his first car, which was unusual in the neighborhood for a boy of his age. It didn't take too long before he had enough saved to buy an old car sufficient for his needs.

One day, around six in the afternoon, he went out to do some shopping in his car and saw Doña Luisa walking in the same direction. She saw him, too, and they greeted each other.

Alfredo slowed down, lowering the window, and said, "Where are you going? Can I take you somewhere?"

Even before receiving an answer, she was sitting in the car.

Alfredo asked, "Where can I take you?"

Her answer surprised him. She said, "Wherever you want."

"I'm going to do some shopping for the store."

"I can go with you. My husband is working the night shift, and he doesn't get home until twelve." Alfredo kept driving, and she asked him, "Have you eaten yet? If you want, we can get something together in a restaurant."

Alfredo suggested a restaurant in the area, but she told him, "No, I don't want to be seen by the neighbors, and I don't want my husband to find out. Why don't we go to the Pan-American? It's close by, there are several nice restaurants, and no one will know us." At the same time, she ran her hand gently over his right leg. "My treat."

On both sides of the Pan-American Highway, there are several hotels often used by lovers, which could be rented by the hour. They were very easy to identify because of their bright neon lights inviting you to visit them.

She asked sarcastically, "Have you ever been here with any of your girlfriends? This place is incredible. Some of the rooms have sound like it's raining, and sometimes they have vibrating beds and whirlpool baths with fancy lights, and sometimes even mirrors on the ceiling. You have to see it."

"No, I've never been here before," he said.

"If you're interested, let me show you. Just so you can see one of those rooms yourself and then tell your friends about it."

"It seems like you've been here before?"

"Oh yes, I've seen them all."

Things were getting even more exciting, and she got closer to him in the car, and said, "Now that we're alone, you can call me Luli."

In less than ten minutes, they had entered the Hotel Jardines de Babilonia, one of the most beautiful in the area. The room was very spacious with a whirlpool tub and a minibar, soft lights, and soft music. As soon as they entered, Luisa went right to the hot tub, undressing as she filled it, and invited him to join her. Her plans were now pretty clear to Alfredo, and Raúl whispered to him from within, *"Beware! The chubby one is going to kill you!"*

Alfredo wasted no time in the hot tub and was soon kissing her breasts passionately. He had waited a long time for this moment. Luli took control, slowed him down, wanting to show him how to satisfy a woman. Alfredo was getting his first sex lesson from a private tutor.

When they were finished, they had both forgotten about dinner and the shopping. They agreed to meet each other on Wednesdays, when her husband was working nights.

That night in bed, Alfredo felt like he was floating on a magic carpet. He couldn't sleep thinking about the plans for next Wednesday.

. . .

The next day, he had difficulties concentrating on his job; it was especially hard looking after a group of young girls of his own age, while trying to not to think about the experience of the night before. Those young girls always came to the store when they knew he would be there, and they dressed up and wore makeup specially to impress him. Often, they would "forget" to buy something on their list as an excuse to return to the store. One day, Alfredo gathered up enough courage to ask one of them, "Analia, would you like to go to the movies with me tonight?"

The schedule for that night at the local theater was a romantic film. Seemingly without even paying attention to the name of the movie, she responded quickly, "Sure, what time do you want to meet?"

Alfredo was taken by surprise because she had accepted so quickly and without asking any questions. She paused, and then she added, "Would you like to go for a drink before going to the cinema?"

He agreed, but when he started to think about it, he got anxious because he didn't know what he was going to talk about. His main topic of conversation would have to be something related to the store, but it didn't seem very interesting to talk to her about the price of oil or the results of last Sunday's football game. Anxiety and panic were no strangers to Alfredo. In only seconds, old anxieties returned.

Alfredo dressed in his best clothes and brought fresh breath mint pills.

When his parents saw him so well dressed, they asked him, "Are you going out?"

He didn't answer with specifics because he and Analia had agreed to keep it a secret. When they finally got together at the train station as they had arranged, she also dressed up as if she was going to a wedding, with beautiful makeup and a sweet perfume. Alfredo was nearly speechless, but managed, "You look great!"

Conversation was easier than he thought. He told her of his plans to expand his business, buy other stores, and transform them into a chain of mini-markets that would soon become the best in Buenos Aires.

Analia flattered him for such ambitious plans.

Alfredo grew more confident minute by minute; what she was saying was music to his ears. It made him feel very important.

Alfredo showed his best side to her and made a very good impression overall.

He felt her listening attentively, and so he kept talking about himself, barely giving her an opportunity to speak. By the time they got into the cinema, they felt very comfortable with each other, and as soon as the lights went out, they began kissing and touching each other, leaving no place unexplored. Doña Luisa's lessons were proving to be very useful.

After that trip to the movies their relationship stopped being a secret; there was hardly a day when they didn't see each other. They made frequent trips to the park in the evening, staying until very late, even though her mother would nag and complain when she got home.

During the first six months of dating Analia, Alfredo kept his Wednesday outings with Doña Luisa a secret, but it was getting harder and harder. One Wednesday, he didn't show for his date with Doña Luisa. It wasn't a surprise then that his first client on Thursday morning was Doña Luisa. She was angry at him for being stood up. Alfredo was afraid of her, and in order to avoid a scene in front of the clients, he took her back to the private office to explain his situation. That didn't satisfy her at all, and to scare him even more, she said, "I'm going to talk to my lawyer and tell him that you have sexually abused me."

Doña Luisa didn't know that Raúl, Alfredo's pécora, was a brilliant lawyer who whispered advice to Alfredo and said, "First of all, you have to deny everything she says. She has no evidence or photos or witnesses, and if she talks, she will be the one who is at risk because her husband will kick her out of the house and she'll end up on the street."

Sometimes it helps to know a lawyer.

Of course, she never followed through on any of her threats, and they went back to the hotel the following Wednesday as usual.

The only conflict in Analia and Alfredo's romance was his jealousy, even though she never gave him anything to be jealous about. This was a product of his insecurity that still remained from his original personality, despite all the encouragement he received from Raúl.

After two years of dating Analía, they started talking about marriage. Alfredo's extravagant fantasies were endless; he talked about new supermarkets, a huge house, a car for each of them, and exotic vacations. It was difficult for her to ignore these promises.

When they did finally get married, the wedding was attended by family members, customers of the store, friends and neighbors, even Doña Luisa. The party lasted almost all night. It was held in the local Community Social Centre, the only place in their neighborhood that could accommodate so many people.

Alfredo had taken complete control of the management of the store when his parents retired, even though they continued to show up every day at the store with the intention of helping. His parents had moved to a small apartment near the store. Alfredo had bought another store that he renovated and converted into another mini market—he was becoming financially independent.

His business succeeded quickly, thanks to the advice from Raúl the pécora that encouraged him to move forward, perhaps faster than he wanted. He soon realized that he could be the best, even better than Raúl.

His future was bright.

Chapter 7

The pécora of Norberto, the bully and dishonest union leader, wandered around for a while before he could find his shell. It seemed that because of his unlikeable personality, he was rejected by all the shells that were available. But time healed all wounds, and finally he penetrated Ricardo, a young boy who was overprotected and controlled by his parents and had very little knowledge of the real world.

Ricardo was tall, blond, with good manners. He had finished high school, was a good student, and was going to continue studying to become an engineer. Perhaps what was unusual was that Ricardo and his family were fervent members of the Divine Belief.

These new congregations had grown a lot in recent years and most of them had developed as a split from traditional religions like Catholicism. Many new recruits to these cults occurred in moments of vulnerability, such as the death of a relative, loss of a job, a long illness, or separation from a partner. They are promised unconditional support, at least initially. Other recruits came because they were disappointed with their current beliefs and were looking for something new.

Like many leaders of groups like these, the cult leaders all had a strong charisma and a special authority that, according to them, was given to them by God. They were able to attract members who accepted their conditions without asking too many questions. Sometimes this unlimited power could generate a fanaticism that was capable of making them dangerous.

Like other members, Ricardo accepted strict rules— asking permission to get married and with whom, what kind of friends he could have. Growing up in such an environment caused a huge impact on Ricardo's behavior. Without noticing, he had become an ardent defender of everything that the cult demanded. He faithfully obeyed his parents and participated in all the activities organized by the group's pastor.

Like many similar organizations, they operated in total secrecy. All the members had overly high opinions of themselves because they truly believed they had been selected by God. This isolated them even more from the outside world and further encouraged a close community life.

The leaders enforced control of the members, causing a feeling of guilt in those who didn't follow all their rules.

For many, the word "cult," or "sect," is associated with sinister ideas, but for others with family, drug, or debt problems, belonging to a cult can be helpful. Those who join the cult soon learn the obligations they have as part the group, including many volunteer jobs and many financial obligations.

During Sunday celebrations, the pastor of Divine Belief never forgot to ask for money, and members knew that they were expected to donate ten percent of their salaries and knew that this would be monitored by accountants who investigated everyone's finances.

When Norberto, Ricardo's pécora, heard the constant requests for money, he murmured, "These people are more corrupt than I am, and they seem to do it without any hesitation at all. They are criminals, and yet no one holds them accountable. I need to learn how to do this, how to be corrupt without anyone noticing."

Ricardo, following a family tradition, had joined the group without arguing with his parents. For him, belonging to the sect gave him a sense of security. He was part of the youth group and tried to look just like everyone else, with a clean look and always short and well-combed hair. They didn't smoke or drink alcohol, and sex was prohibited until the day of their weddings. They all got married to other members of the group.

The combination of Norberto the pécora with Ricardo's shell was as incompatible as oil and water. The internal struggles between the two were constant; Norberto tried to corrupt him but Ricardo, for now, remained faithful to his religious dogmas. Despite these fights, Ricardo was able to continue his studies undisturbed and soon graduated.

Every day, returning from classes at the University, Norberto tempted him with worldly pleasures. As always, he would say, "You need to try a joint. It's very relaxing," or sometimes, "Have you ever slept with a woman?"

He put on a lot of pressure and finally convinced him to go to a bar.

"I've never even tried alcohol," Ricardo said.

"There's always a first time!"

"What happens if my parents or the pastor find out?"

"Don't worry about it. Nobody's going to say anything."

Finally, one day, on his way home from the University, he got off the bus and went to the bar. It was a poorly maintained old house with windows that were painted black so that you couldn't see what was going on inside.

As he was entering the bar, he said to his pécora, "My legs are shaking."

Once inside, he covered his face so that no one would recognize him. His first impression of the place was just like the image he had of hell: a hot, toxic place with nauseating odors, bodies that moved with difficulty, screaming and arguing. Nobody cared what was being said; they only cared about having enough money for the next drink. The yellowed walls were stained by nicotine and dirty handprints from stumbling patrons. The walls were covered old stained beer and liquor advertisements.

The cigarette smoke was so intense that he felt like he was inside a cloud. He saw people walking around with glasses full of liquor, but it was impossible to recognize any faces. That made him feel more comfortable because he knew nobody would recognize him. As he sat on a bench in the bar, an old bartender, with a white beard and a lit cigarette in the corner of his mouth, came over and offered him a drink.

"Yes, please. A glass of sparkling water."

The man was surprised and asked, "Anything else?"

"Yes, with lemon and ice, please."

When Norberto heard this request, he almost exploded, but he thought that maybe it was a good start, given that it was just Ricardo's first time.

While he was drinking the water, some parishioners came to talk to him, but because of their tone of voice and the noise of the bar, he didn't understand a word. He felt very uncomfortable, and that made him even more nervous, and he wanted to leave, despite Norberto's insistence to ask for a real drink.

He left without telling anyone and ran to the bus stop to return home. Although he imagined everyone was watching, no one even noticed.

. . .

What he hadn't expected was that his parents would be waiting for him at the door, worried that he was arriving an hour later than usual.

His mother, almost crying, asked, "What happened? Why didn't you call us?"

His father said, "Where have you been?" And at that moment, his father noticed a strong smell of tobacco. "Have you been smoking? The pastor will find out about this, and you will have to pay for your disobedience. It is a shame for our family."

"No, Dad, I swear I didn't do anything bad. On the bus, I was surrounded by smokers."

They sent him to bathe, to put his clothes in the washing machine, and to sleep without having dinner. Ricardo's relationship with his parents was harmonious because he always obeyed, but tonight's circumstances were very different, and his mother, who had never raised her voice, became hysterical just thinking that her son could have been smoking. His father, as head of the family and wanting to impose his control, forced him the next day to confess his dishonest behavior to the pastor. This was very humiliating for a man who was almost twenty-four years old.

The pastor was intimidating just by his presence, because he was tall, with broad shoulders and stern movements. His penetrating gaze was like a dagger to somebody who had broken some rules.

Those who don't fulfill the mandates of the cult or who try to leave the group would be shunned to the point that they would suffer mental anguish so intense, they would often need psychiatric help.

. . .

Sunday services were something very special. All were smiling, and dressed in their best clothes, and the ceremony began with sacred music that Norberto found very boring.

He said, "This is very different from the tangos that I used to hear in the dance halls and nightclubs on the weekends.

Every time the pastor made an announcement, the members raised their arms and shouted, "Hallelujah!

Hallelujah!" This happened even if the pastor asked for more money because the roof of the church needed to be fixed or anything else—he always seemed to have a good reason.

At the end of the service, there was a procession of people who seemed to be unwell, who walked with difficulty and approached the altar where the pastor received them and spoke to them in a strange language, hit their foreheads, and said, "You are healed!"

They seemed to experience almost epileptic seizures and miraculously began to walk normally.

"Hallelujah! Hallelujah!" they all shouted, making a deafening noise.

Norberto the pécora didn't understand any of this and said, "This seems like witchcraft to me. Are you going to tell me that he just touches you and cures you? If this is true, I am going to bring all the cripples of my neighborhood to see if he can make them walk again."

As usual on all Sundays, the leader reminded all members to be on their best behavior because there was always someone watching them. As he said this, he looked directly at Ricardo in the front row, as if reminding him that his adventure at the bar had not been forgotten.

. . .

It had been three years since Ricardo had a girlfriend. Virginia had said they were the same age, but they had gone to different schools. She was blonde with an innocent face, blue eyes, full lips, a nice tight body fashioned by her gymnastics classes, with small, perky breasts that she exhibited with pride. She was also a member of the youth group that participated in voluntary activities assigned by the cult, and as a reward for so much work, they were invited to the church's cinema once a week. Of course, the films had been carefully screened by the pastor and the elders of the community.

Actually, Ricardo and Virginia had known each other since they were toddlers, because her parents had belonged to the same religious group and they were neighbors. All these years as they grew, their parents said, "Look what a beautiful couple they make!"—even though they were only three years old.

Many times, in kindergarten they would walk together holding hands, sharing toys and the food they had brought to school. The suggestion that they were a couple and that they would eventually get married persisted even until they were teenagers, and they quietly accepted this decision made for them by their parents.

Many weekend dances were organized in the Temple or at the house of one of the cult members, always under the watchful eye of the parents, who didn't allow any body contact while dancing, never mind trying to kiss. It was obvious that teenagers like Ricardo and Virginia were fighting to control their hormones, and to top it off, Ricardo was constantly tortured by his pécora who repeated, "Touch her tits, and she'll go crazy!"

At night in bed, Ricardo couldn't stop thinking about touching his girlfriend's breasts, but he was never able to find an opportunity. They were always being watched. *"Touch the tits!"* echoed in his ears every morning and every night.

Those thoughts tortured him. He could never find peace, and he couldn't confide in anyone. One day, Ricardo couldn't take it anymore, and when leaving one of the youth group meetings, he approached Virginia to say something in her ear, and as soon as he got close to her, he "accidentally" bumped into her breast. At first, there was no reaction at all, and then suddenly, Virginia started crying and left without saying goodbye. They didn't talk or even look at each other for five days. Virginia didn't know that it was Norberto the pécora who had insisted that Ricardo touch her.

To escape from these ideas, Ricardo worked harder and harder to get his diploma. He was obsessive and would study until he fell asleep on top of the books. Studying was the only time he could find any peace.

For Norberto the pécora, there was no difference between evil and good. He had never learned. It was easier to be bad than to be good.

Norberto thought, *I'm sure Ricardo will feel very good if he has a drink and then screws Virginia.*

Ricardo struggled not to show any of that inner struggle, but sometimes he thought about it and realized: *this world is very boring.*

But despite these conflicts that tormented him, he said to Norberto, "No, I don't want to hear you. Please, leave me alone!"

This constant pestering from Norberto tormented Ricardo and caused him great anxiety.

And Norberto insisted, "Touch her tits! Touch her tits!"

. . .

When Ricardo finally graduated as a civil engineer, he had excellent marks, and his future father-in-law appointed him to a position in his construction company. He was going to be in charge of supervising and visiting the construction sites and also buying materials. Pécora Norberto saw in this job an opportunity to defraud both the buyers and the sellers, with the idea of getting rich. This was his specialty. Ricardo could not have had a better teacher.

Norberto pressed Ricardo again and explained the double-dipping technique. "When you make a purchase, ask for a receipt for double what you pay, and then sell it to the buyer at the new price, and you can keep the difference."

Ricardo was appalled. "But that's wrong!"

A few months later, he wanted to buy his first car, but the one he liked was way above of his budget. Just as he was signing the purchase of the vehicle, he had to order the purchase of materials for a new building. It was his chance to buy the car he wanted so much. Ricardo wondered what the consequences would be if his father-in-law ever found out.

Norberto told him to stay calm because no one was going to find out. "Everybody has a corrupt side," he said. "I'll tell you that both your father-in-law and the cult leader are just as corrupt."

Ricardo started to realize that it was becoming difficult for him to distinguish between good and evil. Norberto's ideas began to take over. Everyone in the company was impressed with his work ethic, and now he had another incentive to work even harder. He could not escape the addictive power of money.

"This time is the last time; this is the last time," he promised himself, remembering the teachings and possible punishments imposed by the cult on those who committed a sin.

. . .

After a year of work, the pressure to marry Virginia became very strong. Everyone spoke of the future marriage. Their mothers were eager to have grandchildren, and it was no surprise when Ricardo and Virginia finally announced a wedding date.

Of course, both mothers took care of organizing everything: the bride's dress, the menu for the party, the list of guests, the gift registry, and even the details of the honeymoon. It could be said that it was like an arranged marriage, since everyone had always talked about them as a couple.

The advantage for Ricardo and Virginia was that they didn't have to search indefinitely to find a partner; the two families knew each other and luckily got along well. It was good to know that both sets of parents liked both of them.

The religious ceremony, of course, took place in the Temple of Divine Belief and lasted for what seemed like an eternity. It was a spectacularly hot day, and there were many people with crying children. The pastor spoke to them for nearly an hour about their obligations to each other. Everything he said left no room for the marriage to be any fun and didn't take into account the dreams of two young people excited to start a new life.

After the ceremony, the party was held in a private room, decorated by the mothers of the bride and groom with flowers and gifts for the guests. The seats of the guests had been carefully assigned, separating those who were not members of the cult. The difference between those who belonged and those relatives who didn't was made obvious during the speeches.

The parents' gift to the couple was a house in a closed community called Country Club. This lifestyle had become popular in the 1970s, and most of these communities were far from the big city. The two families were very prosperous and wanted the grandchildren to grow up away from the city in a green and healthy environment. It was reassuring for the parents to know that several members of the cult had a house in the same country club.

The new couple had already decided that Virginia would not work outside the home and would be exclusively dedicated to the care of the house, the husband, and the children to come.

After the honeymoon in Córdoba, they settled into their new home. For the first time, they had some freedom without parental supervision. It was such a strange feeling that, for a while, they were immobilized, waiting for orders as they had done in the past.

Virginia was an excellent cook, so Norberto the pécora told Ricardo, "She feeds you well; now it's your job to satisfy her in bed." Norberto insisted, "If you don't do it, then I tell you, somebody else will!"

Ricardo shrugged as if he didn't care. Norberto could not understand Ricardo's attitude, not being interested in such a beautiful wife.

Chapter 8

Virginia and Ricardo loved living in the country surrounded by large green spaces. Virginia said the little houses looked as if they were from children's fairy tales, with white stucco walls and red-tile roofs and colorful well-kept gardens.

All these gated neighborhoods were very similar. Each had a restaurant and a gym, indoor and outdoor swimming pools, a meeting space, and a golf course.

What Ricardo and Virginia didn't realize was that living at the Country Club was like being in a fish tank. There were big and small fish, some attractive, some not so much. Despite these differences, everyone had something at least something in common, allowing them to develop new friendships and a very active social life, even when some of them weren't members of the cult. Interacting with them could be interesting.

Their home was almost too big for two people. It had two floors with four bedrooms on the top floor, a kitchen on the main floor, a separate dining room, and another room just for entertaining company. The parents wanted their grandchildren to have lots of space. They were also sure that the first grandchild would be born exactly nine months after the wedding day, not a day before or a day after. It would have been embarrassing if the new baby was born early, because everyone would talk.

Therefore, nobody was surprised that in the three years they had been married they had two children, both girls. Soon the house was filled with active, noisy kids. In the backyard, there was a pool and a large garden for the children to run.

Right after they moved in, they got invitations from many of the neighbors for coffee or for dinner. Ricardo was not really interested in having an active social life. He liked staying home alone in his house, and when he really couldn't find an excuse, Norberto the pécora would torture him, saying, "This place is full of old farts, but it wouldn't hurt you to go and enjoy a drink."

Ricardo answered, "What—the only way to have fun is by drinking alcohol?"

Norberto ignored the response and continued whispering to him, "Look at that old woman. She has so much makeup she looks like a clown. Ask her what kind of costume she's wearing. And I'll bet you that the blonde with the red dress sleeps with the neighbor across the street. Look at how she looks at him!"

Ricardo said, "Is that the only thing you can talk about?"

Ricardo detested these events, maybe in part because the majority of the members of the neighborhood were older than him.

Even Virginia noticed that Ricardo's character was beginning to change. Sometimes he would get very aggressive, and that was unusual for him. It seemed like he was showing her deeply hidden parts of his personality. He seemed to have gone from being submissive to being angry all the time, and it was getting hard for her to even talk to him.

Ricardo could see this change in himself and cried, "I'm going crazy! I'm going crazy!"

To make matters worse, his only spiritual adviser was the corrupt Norberto, who told him, "Look, your 'brakes' aren't working well. You can't control your emotions, and that's hurting your relationship with everyone around you."

Ricardo worried. "Do you think it's nice for me to get upset with my wife? When I see what I've done, it's too late to fix it, and I feel terrible! Sometimes I just want everything to end, but I don't know how!"

Virginia could see that Ricardo was no longer the same. She didn't know what was wrong with him. But she had no one to share these worries with.

Ricardo, on the other hand, couldn't find any peace of mind. These fights with Norberto were making him anxious, on top of his obligations to his growing family and to the demands of his job. Ricardo didn't have any time for recreation or any interest in socializing to relax after the stress of his daily job. The relationship with Virginia had lost some of its intimacy. They hardly talked to each other. They didn't seem to have anything in common to talk about, and neither of them seemed interested in the other's feelings anymore. It appeared as if, now that they'd had their children, the attraction to each other had vanished.

Ricardo's anxiety caused headaches, fatigue, lack of ambition, trouble sleeping, and a feeling of being powerless. He could barely find the strength to work and to participate in the activities of the cult. He had periods of anxiety and depression—not unusual in his family because half of them were chronically depressed. All of them were taking homeopathic remedies that they shared with one another. They were strong believers in magical results. It was especially difficult since the cult didn't allow psychiatric treatment for its members. Ricardo probably needed it and felt like he had no one to discuss his problems with. Each day, he sank further and further into his depression.

Norberto the pécora was also frustrated. He complained that life in the fish tank was like being in prison with only short trips away to the Temple or to buy food. There was no adventure. The only thing he had accomplished was to convince Ricardo to do the "double-dipping" with his billings.

He asked Ricardo, "Tell me if this is the kind of life that you want? If this is all there is, then I'd rather be dead."

Norberto the pécora missed his own family. He missed his friends, the meetings in the neighborhood club, the Sunday barbecues. Like all those who've been reincarnated, he wanted to know about them: how his parents were doing, whether his brothers had continued with his businesses. But what he really wanted to know was who had ordered his assassination.

He thought to himself: *I am sure it was my wife Norma. What has she done with all that cash from the insurance policy?*

The relationship between Norberto the pécora and Ricardo the cáscara wasn't working. Ricardo couldn't understand Norberto's attitude toward life. They were coming from very different worlds, and both of them were miserable.

. . .

Virginia's life was not much better. She sent the girls to school and made lunch for Ricardo to bring to work. She cleaned the house all day. She sometimes had a chance to chat with some neighbors from the Country Club, but she never offered any opinions. She would just nod and smile. If she went to the pool to take care of her daughters, she would just sit in a chair in the shade, never entering the water. The cult wouldn't tolerate seeing a married woman in a public place in a bathing suit.

Every two weeks or so, they had a visit from their parents, but these seemed more like inspections than visits. They didn't leave any part of the house uninspected, and Virginia was left to tolerate their criticism if they found something messy or dirty.

Sometimes their friends from the former youth group came to visit her, and conversations were always about what was going on in the Temple, especially about members whose behaviors didn't follow the rules or who hadn't made their obligatory monthly contributions.

"Did you know that the Echeverria's bought a new car and are six months behind in their payments to our assembly?"

"I heard that they are not up-to-date with the expenses of the Country Club, either."

"What do they spend their money on, anyway?"

During one of those visits, one of her friends said there were rumors that the leader of the sect had been abusing some of the girls, but nobody was allowed to talk about it, and if any of the people affected told the secret, they would be shunned. They would lose everything, family, friends, work, and they would be left to the streets. The leader was untouchable, and everyone liked him and respected him.

. . .

Sometimes, after returning from work or after dinner, Ricardo and Virginia went out for a walk the country roads and saw their girls running or on their bicycles. One time, they met a neighbor who approached them to say, "Hi, my name is Alfredo. I moved here just a few weeks ago. Nice to meet you." Looking at the girls, he said, "What are the names of these cuties?"

Alfredo told them that he moved to the Country Club because he need a quiet place to stay during the business trips that he frequently made to the area. They exchanged telephone numbers and arranged to meet later on that weekend.

He told them that he was a businessman in the food industry and owned several supermarkets. Alfredo said to Virginia that if she needed anything from the supermarket, she could call him, and he would bring it over so she wouldn't even have to leave the house. What he didn't mention was that he was single or that he sometimes had late-night visits from young ladies.

When they said goodbye, Ricardo was upset with Virginia for talking to a stranger who had invaded their privacy by asking the girls' names. Norberto said, "What's wrong with being asked the names of the girls? Don't be such an idiot."

For the first time, Virginia disagreed with Ricardo and said, "I thought he seemed very friendly and maybe we should accept his invitation. If you don't like it, I am sorry, but I will want to go. It's good for the girls to meet other people."

. . .

Alfredo thought of himself as being a typical playboy. He was divorced; he owned several stores that he had converted into mini-markets; he drove convertible sports cars and had changed his surname. It was not Alfredo López anymore, now it was Alfredo López Ponce "the businessman." He had business cards made up with his new information. He had a new girlfriend every week. That was the kind of life that Raúl the pécora wanted. Raúl was very impressed with Alfredo. Raúl even thought that Alfredo was like a better version of himself and was doing everything that he had not been able to do in his own life.

Alfredo was very popular with everyone around him, except for his former wife, Analía.

Analía's vision of Alfredo was different. She said,

"Sometimes he can be charming and generous, but other times he is very selfish and only thinks of himself. When we were married, he didn't care if I caught him in his little sexual escapades. He never cared about my needs, the world always revolved around him."

With Alfredo's new status as an important business person, he gradually lost the ability to enjoy the smaller things. Nothing like that motivated him anymore—a sunrise, a beautiful flower, or the smile of a child. He just couldn't get excited enough to enjoy simple, everyday things.

Chapter 9

As time went on, Ricardo and Virginia met most of their neighbors and noticed that they were usually were very prosperous and that they had moved to the Country Club in search of a change in their lifestyle and a more secure and peaceful environment.

They were generally older, and this worried them a bit, but they also found young families with school-age children who went to the same school as their own girls. The Country Club was a tiny representation of society at large, a society unknown to Ricardo and Virginia. There were divorcees, widowers, single parents, and many couples on their second or third marriages.

But what Ricardo and Virginia didn't expect was the constant traffic between their houses at dusk—people looking for love. And as the new day came, these new couples pretended that they didn't know each other at all, let alone that they had just slept together. The only expectation was that they would have to return to their own places before the local children left for school in the morning, so they could avoid being caught in their indiscretions.

Irene and Felipe were a couple who had just moved into the Country Club. They were in their mid-fifties. She was a sixth-grade elementary school teacher, and he was an accountant for a large construction company. Physically plain, Irene was plump with an unruly mixture of gray hair and dyed blond that urgently needed a touch-up. She didn't pay much attention to her own appearance, although in every other aspect she could be defined as a perfectionist. Any chores she did were always done flawlessly. Fortunately for her, she had recently been reincarnated by someone with a very different personality. But in this situation, Isabel the pécora and Irene the cáscara, instead of fighting, were able to balance the positive values of one another and understood each other very well.

Isabel the pécora told Irene, "I know you try to make everything perfect. There are many women like you who try to be the best wives, the best mothers, the best teachers and still are never satisfied. They say to themselves 'I could have done better' and when they don't succeed, they get frustrated, depressed, and anxious."

When Irene was frustrated, she ate. Cookies mostly. This made her gain extra pounds, and so, she was always trying to lose weight. She had tried all the fashionable diets and knew that after two or three months, they stopped working.

Her husband Felipe was short, skinny, and always looked sickly because of his yellow-gray skin color and receding lower jaw, which made him look very ordinary. It was not uncommon to hear people say, "But Felipe is such a good person! Such a good person!"

Irene and Felipe had two sons and four grandchildren who didn't visit very often. Although Irene didn't say so openly, it was obvious that she didn't tolerate the dirt and disorganization left behind by her grandchildren. After their visits, she spent many hours cleaning and looking for traces of candy on the walls. The most irritating things were finding sticky door handles and books out of place. Books, photo albums or whatever that caught their attention would be moved without worrying about returning them to the original site. She liked it better when she went to visit them in their homes, so she didn't have to worry about cleaning what they messed up, even something insignificant like fingerprints on the windows.

They had saved a good amount of money because they were very organized. With the money from the sale of the apartment they'd owned downtown and some savings of their own, they were able to buy this house in the Country Club and fulfill their dreams. Even so, before moving in, Irene ordered many renovations; she didn't like the floors or the color of the walls.

Felipe and Irene moved to the Country Club when they began to think about retiring.

As a perfectionist, she was always giving orders to Felipe: "You forgot to turn off the bathroom light. You have to clean the car. You forgot to take out the garbage."

On and on. Her list was endless. Felipe was very patient, although it sometimes seemed that when she spoke, he didn't listen to her.

Irene's pécora, Isabel, was the opposite of her perfectionism. She was very relaxed, and instead of imposing her point of view, she tried to help Irene. The two of them had a very cordial relationship. Isabel said to Irene, "You can't do everything perfectly all the time! If you don't do anything until you are sure it will be perfect, you will never do anything at all!" Isabel constantly reminded her, "The one who doesn't risk, doesn't win. No pain, no gain!"

Irene was afraid of new challenges and limited herself to do things only when she felt comfortable. Her specialty was cookies—mostly for personal consumption, but also to give away to her acquaintances. Whoever visited her couldn't leave without taking some of her famous cookies.

One day, Irene proudly told Isabel, her pécora, "I'm going to try something new, even if it doesn't turn out perfectly."

Isabel was surprised and replied, "Very good, very good! Congratulations!"

"I'm going to try a new recipe for the cookies. I have never changed the recipe in the last twenty years!"

Despite Isabel's efforts to make Irene less obsessive, she was so fastidious at home that in her pantry, the cans were all arranged alphabetically. If Felipe rearranged anything and put it where it didn't belong, he would have to listen to her complaints for hours.

Felipe and Irene were devout Catholics. They never missed Mass on Sundays or any other religious celebrations. She volunteered in the church, and when they had a bazaar, she baked cookies to help raise funds. As a teacher, Irene was very strict and dedicated to her work. She was always at school an hour before the other teachers. She demanded perfection from her students. She had a reputation for excellent teaching and strong discipline, and the parents liked that approach. She could have been the school principal, but she had rejected the opportunity several times because she was afraid of such a big responsibility.

Isabel reminded her, "Irene, why don't you want to be the principal?"

"Look, Isabel, I feel safe as a sixth-grade teacher. I know that the kids need me."

She knew that she often felt paralyzed trying to make everything perfect. With Isabel's help, despite her obsession with perfection, she was able to improve her relationships with other people. She quickly adapted to the social life of the Country Club, sharing gardening secrets with other neighbors and even giving away the recipe for her famous cookies.

Some neighbors sent their children to Irene to get help with their homework, especially those who were a little behind in their grades.

In the afternoons, before dinner, she and Felipe sat at the front porch of the house where they greeted passing neighbors and exchanged news. They also went to bingo sessions on Friday nights and accepted all the invitations they received.

They started taking golf lessons, and Irene took it very seriously. In a short time, she was even better than Felipe, and with the help of Isabel, she was encouraged to participate in the women's tournament, even winning the silver medal. Unlike many perfectionists, Irene was happy, probably because she had learned to limit herself to just doing what she felt comfortable with, but also because the new life in the Country Club and the fact that she was soon to retire made her feel even better.

Isabel told her, "Now you have to do things for yourself."

"What do you think if I go to the hairdresser every two weeks?"

"Very good, and you should get a manicure and a pedicure at the same time."

Except for Felipe, everyone noticed the change in Irene's appearance, at least on the surface. But despite these changes, she didn't depart much from her perfectionist profile. Her house remained impeccable, and her perseverance and tenacity led to excellent results in her game of golf.

. . .

Irene's pécora, Isabel, had died in a car accident at the age of eighteen. Even though she was young, people said that she was unusually mature for her age. Because of that, she was frequently asked by her friends for advice when they had problems at school or with their parents or friends. Isabel had been the only daughter of older parents. She was born when her mother was forty-three; her mother had married in her late thirties and it had taken several years to conceive Isabel. Her parents were professors of psychology at the University, and from the time she was a small girl, she was always exposed to complex intellectual conversations, unusual for someone so young.

Her parents had no interest in sports or outdoor life. Their recreation consisted only of reading books and more books. Isabel adapted to that lifestyle without resentment; she was also an avid reader. When she started high school, she surrounded herself with many friends and participated in dances and meetings, but her strength was the ability to help anyone who needed it.

The news of her death had spread through the school like lightning. Her classmates cried and embraced in total disbelief. The school principal suspended classes for two days. As for her parents, it could be said that with the news of her death, they aged a hundred years in just twenty-four hours, and it obvious that their life would never be the same again.

Many reincarnates wanted to get back in touch with their loved ones, but Isabel knew that seeing her parents growing old would depress her, and for that reason, she chose not to see them again, or even to be in contact with her friends. All of them would have formed families of their own by now, and little by little, they would have forgotten her. On the other hand, her relationship with Irene was very pleasant; she felt good, they worked together, and they understood each other in almost everything. Isabel the pécora didn't need to go back to her past.

. . .

In recent months, based on the changes that Irene had experienced, such as settling into the Country Club, playing golf, and improving her physical appearance, Isabel began to pressure Irene to improve her relationship with Felipe.

"You have to get closer to Felipe."

"What do you want me to do?"

"Organize a romantic dinner in a restaurant, just the two of you."

"But sometimes I feel like he's in a coma!"

"Make reservations in a restaurant. Arrive separately. Dress up extra nice and wear lots of makeup."

"I'm sure when he sees me like that, he will get scared and run away."

Isabel ended by saying, "No pain, no gain."

Chapter 10

Purchasing one of the nicest homes in the Country Club was a gay couple, the newest residents in the neighborhood. Miguel (or Miguelito or Mike) was an interior decorator. His partner Antonio, whom they called Anton, owned a successful beauty salon. He had many employees, but he took personal care of actresses and other celebrities, looking after them in a private room or in their own homes.

Mike was tall, blond, and with an inquisitive gaze. Mike made most of the decisions in the relationship, such as vacations, home purchases, and control of bank accounts. Anton was a little bit shorter with a sweet and gentle voice. When they spoke amongst themselves, they used different pet names.

"What do you want to eat tonight, sweetheart?"

"Whatever you want, darling."

In the Country Club, they became popular very quickly. Anton gave advice to the women about the most appropriate haircuts for their ages or about hair coloring that best matched certain skin tones and eye colors.

Mike, for his part, helped their neighbors with decorating their homes, where to buy furniture, what color to paint their rooms, or what kind of curtains to get for the windows. On the other hand, the husbands of these neighboring wives were not very happy because Mike's advice always seemed to cost a lot of money.

Mike and Anton's friendliness facilitated their acceptance by most members of the Country Club, despite the prejudices associated with homosexuality at the time.

Many of those who lived in the neighborhood had been reincarnated, but neither Mike nor Anton had been penetrated by a pécora; they could be said to be virgins, at least in that respect.

By chance, both were born in the sign of Virgo. Their birthdays were in August, and as good Virgos, they were meticulous and efficient in their life and work. They both enjoyed cultured and tasteful things, and both enjoyed a night at a concert or a play. The most interesting thing about them was that because they had not been penetrated by other spirits, they remained happy and innocent like children, without malice or envy.

Their innocence was a simple contrast to other adults, who had become like wild animals, full of envy, prejudice and resentment. Mike and Anton were not religious in the sense of attending any church, but they defined themselves as spiritual and nourished their spirituality with intense meditation sessions. This gave them an inner life that led them to care more about others and not so much for themselves, which made them genuinely happy.

Every time Irene had a chance, she said, "Many 'normal' couples—in other words, heterosexual—don't get along as well as they do," perhaps as a reflection of her own married life.

Talking to Irene, neighbor Alfredo told her, "In English they call them 'gay.' Here we call them 'homosexuals,' 'putos,' 'trolos,' or 'queers.'" And he added, "They might be different but not 'abnormal.' In English, "gay" means "happy," and that's what most impresses me about Mike and Anton. They are happy and they try to spread that happiness to those around them."

Little by little, Mike and Anton were accepted into the community, despite the initial hesitation of the "fishbowl" environment of the Country Club.

Anton and Mike's chalet became the social center for many of the members, and every month, they organized a themed dinner. They also organized a monthly book club. Many Country Club residents came to these parties, although not everyone associated with the couple outside those events.

It was no surprise that Norberto, the corrupt pécora, told Ricardo, "If you make friends with them, I promise that I'll shoot myself in the balls." And he shouted, "I can't take it anymore with all those fags!"

. . .

Over time, another couple moved in to the neighborhood of the Country Club. Diana and Santiago Del Campo each had children from previous marriages who didn't live with them. Diana was not yet fifty years old, but she pretended to look like thirty, and she invested a lot of money in cosmetics, hairdressing, and clothes, working long hours as an executive secretary to pay for her expensive tastes.

As a young girl, Diana had been introverted and aloof; she was always worried about what others thought of her, which limited her socially. She was the typical middle daughter. After finishing high school, she got a job as a receptionist in an office where hundreds of employees sat all day in individual compartments. Diana arrived at eight in the morning and left at four in the afternoon without talking to anyone; she didn't know anyone by name and, quite possibly, nobody except her supervisor knew hers.

Her family was surprised the day she brought home Juan, her first boyfriend, and within a few months, they had announced their intention to get married. She soon became pregnant, and they had two children in quick succession, first a boy and then a girl. Her family thought that the change in her character was due to the burden of having a new family, her job, or an extroverted husband. No one suspected that the changes occurred after being reincarnated by her pécora, Sandra.

Sandra the pécora took control of Diane's personality, and within six months, Diana and Juan had separated. Diana went back to school. She took adult courses specialized in commercial and office management. She got a job in the same company as her original employer and was quickly promoted to be in charge of many of those who only a short time before had been at the same level.

Nobody recognized her anymore because of the transformation she had experienced in her character and her well-groomed appearance. Her personality change was dramatic. In the office, it was now common to see her get easily agitated, and she was very strict, and her employees were universally afraid of her. Although she had an easy smile, everyone thought it was fake. They said, "If you don't do what she wants, she shows you that big smile and then stabs you in the back."

She abused her power by creating conflict and division among her subordinates. Diana was very demanding at home, too, and everyone was wondering how anyone could handle her. Maybe her salary and her looks were enough to attract somebody.

It didn't take her long to get a husband, despite her fragile emotional state. From the time of her separation from Juan until her marriage to Santiago, the number of candidates she attracted was staggering. Her family was confused because by the time they knew one of her boyfriends and could remember his name, she already had another. It was common to hear her declare eternal love and then abruptly abandon a relationship after bitter complaints and fights.

It was hard for some to understand why Santiago ended up marrying her. He had enormous patience, and he was even amused by her exaggerated reactions. However, within a few months of getting married, many times when Santiago approached her romantically, she told him, "I don't feel well. I am very tired. It was an endless day full of meetings." This was a very different Diana than the one that he knew when they were dating, who was always eager.

Diana made a drama of little things, and she could always find a good reason to make a scene every day. Depending on the circumstances, she used a different emotional blackmail if he wouldn't do what she wanted or if she was not the center of his attention. She would start crying inconsolably. It was common to hear her say, "You don't love me anymore"—and that was a guarantee to get what she wanted.

She always wanted to be the center of attention and used a delicate tone with her friends and showered them with compliments and gifts. During parties with friends, she was often heard saying in a gentle voice, "Oh, darling, you are looking so beautiful!" and "I remembered you on my trip to Europe and brought you this little gift. I hope you like it!"

Her friends would ask, "How was your trip?"

"Very nice, but there are so many tourists, you have to wait a long time in line before you can enter the museums, and everything is so expensive!"

Diane established a close personal relationship with Mike and Anton. They understood her and helped her with her issues.

Anton advised her, "I'd like to give your hair a darker tone to enhance your fabulous blue eyes. With your hair a bit shorter, it will make you look even younger!"

This was music to her ears; she cared a lot about her appearance.

Her husband Santiago complained, "Every morning she spends half an hour in the bathroom putting on her makeup."

She would defend herself, saying, "I can't go outside with these dark circles under my eyes. It would be terrible if my employees saw me the way I look when I wake up. I even scare myself when I look in the mirror."

She knew that her exaggerated makeup and sophisticated clothes would make her the center of attention. She even thought about having plastic surgery to enlarge her breasts."

Anton's relationship with Diana was great. It was like having a private model that followed all his advice.

Diana and Santiago joined the Country Club activities and organized parties in their home. Santiago cooked, and Diana received the guests and served the drinks.

The one reason for them to leave the city and move to the Country Club had been the desire to improve their lifestyle. In the city, they were always surrounded by temptations. They ate in restaurants almost daily, and their social life absorbed them and left them with hardly any time for themselves. Once they arrived in the Country Club, they improved their diet, began exercising, and ran several kilometers every day. It was not strange to see them in their expensive workout wear, jogging before going to work.

Chapter 11

One Saturday during the summer, Mike and Anton organized a dinner for a few neighbors. They sent very beautiful handwritten invitations: "Come and share a night in Spain."

The menu consisted of traditional Spanish meals, and each couple was asked to bring some tapas to share. They also suggested dressing in Spanish costumes, although Mike and Anton were the only ones who did—one of them with a typical beret from the Basque country, and the other a bullfighter.

They sent invitations to:

- Alfredo and companion (they were never sure who would be his date)
- Virginia and Ricardo
- Irene and Felipe
- Diana and Santiago

They also invited five other neighbors, including a retired military officer who called himself "General," although everyone suspected that he had never actually reached that rank. It was easy to identify him by his forceful gestures and his way of walking as if he was in a military parade. His wife always followed him a few steps further back.

The other guests were an accountant, an artist, and two university professors.

Their unofficial guest list was different. No one saw it. It looked something like this:

- Alfredo the perverted narcissist, and his whore of the day
- Ricardo the corrupt, faithful member of the cult, and Virginia
- Irene the finicky and Felipe the airhead
- Diana the dramatic and Santiago the obedient.

Alfredo accepted the invitation immediately. He explained that he was not an expert in the kitchen because he was always surrounded by women who cooked for him and had a maid, but he offered to bring products from his supermarkets, including prosciutto, olives, cheese, and wine. He added that he would be accompanied by a young lady but didn't add any details. He took care of the drinks and sent several boxes of Rioja wine, a very popular Spanish wine and a good complement for tapas. Alfredo brought everything to them a few days before the party. Mike and Anton could not believe how much he brought— it was enough food to feed a hundred insatiable gluttons.

Mike and Anton had spent hours decorating the house with posters: one announcing a bullfight, another with a map of Spain and its different regions and others with flamenco dancers. They cooked a variety of tapas, Galician octopus, garlic prawns, melon and ham sandwiches, toast with camembert and walnuts and some casseroles with chickpeas and cod.

The table was elaborately decorated with brightly colored napkins on each plate, small vases with daisies, and candles that gave off a sweet and intoxicating aroma. All over the house, you could hear very soft classical Spanish guitars, including the Aranjuez concert by Rodrigo, "Bolero" by Ravel and music of Albéniz. Upon arrival, the ladies received a fan with the colors of the Spanish flag to cool off on that hot summer night.

Mike and Anton were in charge of the formal presentations. Everyone was a little tense at the beginning, and eager to meet each other, and their conversations were at first rather trivial. Ricardo and Virginia were anxious because they had never participated in a party like this. Norberto the pécora of Ricardo was excited to see the wine boxes and said, "Tonight, I'm going to drink until I pass out. These fags can really organize a party—you should learn from them."

Diana, following Anton's advice, had put on a very short skirt and wore a blouse with neckline so low-cut that you could see her bra; it was very provocative, almost too much for this kind of neighborhood party.

When Alfredo the perverted narcissist conqueror saw her, he jumped to talk to her without even acknowledging Santiago or his own date. He tried to impress her by talking about his business. "I have a chain of supermarkets and I'm about to open one very close to here."

Diana, who was not going to miss the opportunity to show her talents, answered, "Alfredo, my specialty is human resources and marketing, but I am a little tired of my current job. I would love to try something new!"

"My supermarkets are the best and my motto is, 'High-class supermarkets for everyone.' I'm sending all the competitors into bankruptcy. I would love you to visit our business and see if there is any possibility we could work together."

Alfredo's date for that the night didn't understand anything that was going on. She had never eaten that type of food, she wondered about the decorations, and didn't know anything about Spain.

She asked Alfredo, "What is Spain, a soccer team?"

Alfredo knew that it would be useless to try to explain and said, "Sure, it's a soccer team and a very good one."

To himself, he said, "I hope that she is smarter in bed!"

The General lost no opportunity to tell everybody about his adventures in the army, even though most of his career had been spent behind a desk. He competed with Diana for the attention of the rest of the group, but her cleavage captured everyone's interest.

Of course, Irene the Finicky arrived with three trays of delicious tapas. She was a fantastic cook, and everything looked extremely appetizing.

Diana asked Ricardo and Virginia about their daughters. "Where are those beauties? I have to congratulate you; they are so polite!"

Virginia told her that her mother had taken them to sleep at her house and would bring them back the next day.

"That's great! It's great to get a babysitter. As a young couple, you need a bit of space for yourself. If you ever need me to take care of the girls, I will be delighted to look after them!"

Just then, their host Mike approached with drinks. "You have to taste this 'nectar' of grapes."

Nectar of grapes sounded like fruit juice, and no one imagined that it could be an alcoholic drink. Because of the spicy food, the Spanish chorizo, and other delicacies, the "nectar of grape" was quite enjoyable. Ricardo and Virginia also did not suspect and drank a lot of it through the night. Norberto didn't say anything about it at all; he didn't want them to know that they were drinking alcohol and was happy to see them so relaxed.

With the help of the Rioja, the guests relaxed over time, and their conversations became more interesting. There was laughter throughout the house. Diana the Dramatic came up to Irene and said in her usually exaggerated manner, "I really must congratulate you for your garden, you have to share your secrets with me."

"Simple. My secret is to water the plants every single day."

By this time, Felipe was also drinking and had lost his usual shyness and spoke up for the first time. "Diana, the real secret is that she talks to her plants. I often see her walking through the garden talking to the plants as if they were family."

As the good hosts they were, Mike and Anton took pains to make everyone feel at home. People circulated from one room to another; tapas and drinks were served everywhere, and everybody felt as if they were old friends. No one seemed to want to leave, even though it was already late.

Alfredo was the first to leave; he had other business in mind with his new date.

Irene offered to help them clean up the house, but Mike and Anton said they would deal with it in the morning.

Diana didn't know how to thank them. "My dears, this was the best party I've been to since I was eighteen. I loved the tapas and the Rioja wine. It's my new favorite. We should rotate between our houses next time. It's such a lot of work!"

Mike and Anton answered together, "We loved having you guys over. Everybody was so nice!"

Ricardo and Virginia were the last to leave. They almost didn't say goodbye, not because they did not want to, but because they couldn't. They had been drinking wine for the first time and had quite a lot. This was very new to them, and they were delighted.

Norberto, the pécora of Ricardo, couldn't believe what had happened. He had always tried to encourage him to drink, but this time Ricardo had done it all on his own. He had forgotten the rules of the cult, and now he felt very good.

Ricardo and Virginia had a lot of trouble finding their way home. In the darkness, the streets of the Country Club seemed to have transformed into a labyrinth, and all the houses looked nearly identical. They walked for more than half an hour without recognizing their own. They walked with difficulty, staggering, holding each other to avoid falling. When they finally found the house, Virginia, who had the keys, tried to open the door several times without success. She told Ricardo. "It seems to me that the hole in the lock has shrunk."

Ricardo, with his engineer's mind, replied, "That's impossible. Here, let me try." Finally, in an authoritative voice, he said, "No, I think that the key has gotten bigger!"

Unable to unlock the door, they went to the back of the house and crept in through a window that had been left open, but they never made it to their bed. Instead, they dropped themselves on the floor of the living room and slept uninterrupted for eight hours. They woke up just minutes before their parents came back with the girls but weren't completely able to hide the traces of the previous night. The strong smell of wine on their breaths gave them away.

The grandparents didn't say a word but tried to take the girls back to their house because they didn't think Virginia and Ricardo would be able to take care of them. They reproached them for not going to the Sunday celebration in the Temple. Ricardo and Virginia said nothing but felt like their heads were going to explode. Every little noise bothered them.

The grandparents left without saying anything more. Of course, Ricardo and Virginia knew that their behavior would not soon be forgotten.

Mike and Anton's party had been so successful that when all the other residents of the Country Club learned about it, they wanted to be invited to the next party, which was already being organized—this time with an Italian theme.

Chapter 12

Jesus said to the crowds, "I came to bring fire to the earth, and how I wish it were already kindled! I have a baptism with which to be baptized, and what stress I am under until it is completed! Do you think that I have come to bring peace to the earth? No, I tell you, but rather division! From now on five in one household will be divided, three against two and two against three; they will be divided: father against son and son against father, mother against daughter and daughter against mother, mother-in-law against her daughter-in-law and daughter-in-law against mother-in-law."
(Luke 12:49-53)

Virginia and Ricardo were overwhelmed with obligations as a family with young girls; the Country Club activities, new friendships, and the distance to the Temple were straining their relationship. These activities kept them away from their families and, even worse, from their participation in the activities of their religious group.

They were also openly critical of the leader's plans to build a new Temple to accommodate three thousand believers per service. That would increase the number of participants but, more importantly, increase the financial gains of the greedy leader of the group,

Virginia complained, "Today a letter arrived detailing the budget for the construction of the new Temple, requiring an increase in the members' monthly tithing, increasing up to twenty-five percent of everyone's monthly salaries. It will be impossible for us to contribute this amount without sacrificing some of our essential expenses!"

Ricardo usually tried to avoid confrontations, and he said. "Don't worry. We'll find some way to solve this problem."

In his mind, Ricardo knew he would have to keep "double-dipping" on his billings or give up the cult and suffer the consequences. To help cope with all the expenses of the family, Virginia had decided to get a job; Ricardo's regular salary was not enough. They needed something more.

To complicate things, Norberto the pécora insisted to Ricardo, "Remember what a wonderful time you had at Mike and Anton's party? The cult is obsolete! You need to learn to enjoy life! You really need to learn to enjoy life!"

Ricardo felt like a hypocrite because he kept "double-dipping" on his accounts, but Norberto repeated, "You're like Robin Hood; you take from the rich to give to the poor." Obviously in this case the "poor man" was Ricardo himself.

Ricardo had started "double-dipping" whenever they needed money for unexpected expenses—like sending the girls to summer camp or paying for piano lessons.

Virginia had also changed. She began to attend gym classes at the club, and her silhouette was going back to the way she was before she got married. She enjoyed meeting with the other young mothers in the club and especially enjoyed the interesting conversations about things she'd never even thought about before.

It would be wrong to say that only the men talked about sex and their wild fantasies. In truth, when the women talked about sex, they did it without bragging or inhibitions, and in even more depth than men.

They discussed how to achieve orgasm, how to fake one, how best to find pleasure, and even sex toys. All this for Virginia was a revelation.

She began to organize reunions in her house with her new friends and was surprised at how much they had in common. She started changing her clothing, with more modern and colorful outfits. She realized that there was much more than what the cult preached. She said to herself, "I am young, and I want to have a full life even if that means separating from everyone."

On the contrary, Ricardo felt imprisoned living between two worlds. The only way he could get rid of the mental torture that burdened him was by sleeping or walking by himself very early in the morning before Virginia and the girls got up. He didn't know what to do; the cult was always watching.

Norberto was harassing him constantly to leave the sect, and Ricardo felt guilty as he recognized that his own corruption was already part of his life. To make matters worse, he hardly spoke with Virginia anymore. Their married life wasn't working; they were like two separate entities. This depressed him even more. He was confused, and he didn't know how to escape from this prison.

Sometimes the brain makes decisions without listening to the heart, and in Ricardo's case his decisions had to pass through Norberto's approval, and that made everything more difficult. Virginia also urged him to stand firm and free himself from his parents' interference in order to live as independent adults.

After that famous party at Mike and Anton, both Virginia and Ricardo's parents found out even more details of the party, and the four of them decided to go to their house to confront them. They arranged to see them over the weekend, and when they arrived at the house, there was no doubt that it was going to turn into a confrontation.

Ricardo's father began with a strong tone. "What we saw the other day was disgusting, both of you were drunk. And now we find out that the owners of the house where the party was held are homosexuals! Have you even thought about how this will affect your daughters? They are our granddaughters, and we will not allow anything like this to happen to them."

Ricardo's mother yelled at Virginia, "It's a shame what you have done, the example you have given. You should know that it's your job as the 'woman' to maintain the traditions in your family. You aren't the sweet and innocent girl we used to know. And this is not just me saying this;

your own parents are very disappointed with you, too!"

Not to be outdone, Virginia's father told Ricardo, who still didn't dare to speak, "My wife and I have no doubt that the night of the party you drank too much, disobeying the basic rules of our religious dogma and our family principles. And besides that, in the office, several of my oldest employees have complained about the way you've been treating them."

Ricardo panicked that someone might have discovered his financial cheating.

Virginia's father continued. "This has caused us great pain and disappointment. We have talked about it, and we have decided on the changes you'll have to make before we can have confidence in both of you again. You have ninety days to clean up your act." He gave each of them a copy with a list of rules they had to follow:

- No parties where alcohol is served.
- Attend celebrations every Sunday at the Temple.
- Never socialize with the homosexuals again.
- Switch the girls to our school. We'll pay for the transportation for the girls from the Country Club.
- We'll choose the clothes that Virginia will be allowed to wear in order to regain respectability.
- We'll supervise your finances to ensure you comply with all your tithing obligations for the

Temple.

• We will be back in ninety days to verify that you complied with all of this. Otherwise, we will recommend that you should be expelled from the Temple.

But when their parents left, Ricardo and Virginia knew that even if they accepted all their demands, their relationship with their parents would never be the same. Without a doubt, this manipulation was typical of the cult! Control, control, and more control. That was how they worked.

Virginia was furious and clearly told Ricardo that she wouldn't tolerate this kind of interference in her private life, but Ricardo was not ready to defy them as she suggested; he was afraid of the consequences of separating from his parents.

"I'm tired of being treated like kids. We are old enough to make our own decisions." Looking at the list of recommendations left to them by the parents, she said, "Where do they get off trying to separate the girls from their friends from school, or telling me how I should dress? At my age! I was surprised that they didn't tell us how we should behave in the bedroom!"—and she added sarcastically—"I would have told them that, in that respect, they shouldn't worry because we are like brother and sister.

"There are two possibilities: accept their demands or change completely and separate us from the cult and from them. If we do that, I know it will be very difficult at the beginning, but in the end, we will be a lot happier."

This caused Ricardo a lot of anxiety, and to top it off, Norberto kept telling him, "Tell your parents to go to hell! They are the problem!"

The following weeks were going to be very difficult. They had decisions to make and parents to talk to. That night, they were both exhausted and decided to go to bed—although Ricardo stayed awake most of the night.

The next day, it was clear to them that, through the parents, the cult wanted to impose CONTROL, CONTROL, and more CONTROL, and that they would have to submit to the demands of the leader who considered himself a prophet of God.

The cult controlled its followers in all aspects of their lives, including the way they dressed, their activities, finances, relationships, and possessions. The leader decided who you can see, what you can do, what you can say, and how you should say it. The faithful were obliged to obey these rules without exceptions. Control was exercised through fear. The members were told that the punishments for not satisfying God or even the leader would be rejection and Hell. Fear and threats were the weapons used to keep members loyal.

Ricardo and Virginia knew that they could not ask any questions or try to modify any of the rules already established by the leader. If they separated from the cult, their parents would no longer be able to see their granddaughters. Virginia thought that would be a useful tool in negotiating a settlement with her parents.

Chapter 13

Alfredo prided himself on his ability to attract younger women. He knew they thought of him as a "sugar daddy." But in reality, many others just thought of him as a dirty old man with a thick wallet.

He wasn't the only gray-haired old guy with morning joint pains who started up relationships with girls the age of their own daughters. Some got married and had children who were the same age as their grandchildren, causing confusion because their grandchildren might play with their uncles and have brothers or sisters thirty years younger than them. Sometimes the daughters couldn't stand the new "mother," who also had a better figure than they did.

This was not a problem for Alfredo because he had no intentions of marrying, he didn't have any daughters, and he was not planning to have children either, even though he knew the young girls that he was dating all dreamed of having babies.

But Pécora Raúl did have daughters, and he was desperate to see them and to know about their lives. He suspected that they would have been married by now, maybe even had children, and Raúl was fascinated by that idea.

He was also interested in knowing about Susana, his wife, whom he imagined had even more cosmetic surgeries, wore even more makeup and more provocative clothes, and by now was sleeping with all the lawyers in his firm. He knew that many of them wanted to take her to bed, and he wondered, *Has she remarried? How many lovers has she had?*

He was pretty sure that she would not be alone for lack of potential suitors, but he wanted to know more details.

He wanted to get close to them, but he didn't know where to start. It occurred to him to go to Récoleta, the neighborhood where his apartment had been and where his children went to the school and had their friends. He thought that because they liked the area so much, he might stay in the same area and live nearby.

Récoleta was one of the most prestigious neighborhoods of Buenos Aires, built between 1920 and 1940 when Argentina was the breadbasket of the world and its coffers were full of gold. The luxurious buildings had a very Parisian style, and the Porteños never missed the opportunity to point out that Buenos Aires was the Paris of South America. The highlight of this neighborhood was the Lady of Pilar Basilica and the Récoleta cemetery that housed the remains of many presidents, artists and anyone who had money enough to pay for a mausoleum.

As it was, the only possibility for Raúl to get close to his family was to convince Alfredo to walk every afternoon around Récoleta and take a table on the sidewalk in the open-air restaurants to spend hours drinking espresso, hoping that one day they might pass by and that he would be able to recognize them.

He also said to Alfredo, "Would you please ask the neighbors if they know anybody in my family?"

But Alfredo was uncomfortable approaching strangers and playing the role of a detective. He tried two or three times to approach the neighbors and ask them questions, but they always looked at him with suspicion. Even so, Raúl was not willing to give up. They spent months in the same routine, walking around the neighborhood and drinking coffee. This always put Alfredo in a bad mood, taking away time from his business and interfering with his dating.

During one of those walks, Raúl convinced him to talk to the doorman of his old apartment in Paraná and Juncal in front of the Plaza Vicente López.

Don Francisco, the doorman of his building, was a beefy Galician who wore two different uniforms—one for the morning with gray pants, khaki shirt, and boots, when he was cleaning the corridors, the sidewalk and, of course, polishing the bronze doors handles; and one for the afternoon when he would stand in the front door like a soldier in the army wearing a more formal uniform: a dark green suit with gold buttons, white shirt, and a black bow tie. In the afternoon, his job was to greet everyone as they came and went: he opened the door and greeted them respectfully and helped them with their packages and suitcases. Even more important was to exchange information with the other doormen from neighboring buildings about what was going on with the tenants of his building:

"Did you know that the Garcia's are separating?"

"I think the Duhalde's are having money problems—this year there is no summer vacation for them, and they hardly ever give tips anymore."

Raúl was sure that Don Francisco was the only one who might know what was going on with his family. For months and months, Raúl and Alfredo continued with the same routine: walks through Récoleta neighborhood, with many hours quietly drinking espressos. His favorite observation post was at an outdoor table in the garden of La Biela Restaurant, a classical rendezvous. Raúl always chose that spot, hoping that his family still lived in the area. He imagined that at some point he would see them and insisted on continuing to search and watch.

La Biela was the social center of the residents of Récoleta. It was a common meeting place for intellectuals as well as for business and romantic encounters. A classic eatery, the waiters attended the customers as if they were part of the family. Before long, they were calling him "Don Alfredo"— he was very popular with the waiters. He was friendly with them and left generous tips—they always had a table for him, even if the place was full.

On more than one occasion, Alfredo followed the wrong person, thinking they might be one of Raúl's daughters. Raúl believed that even though it had been several years since his death, he would still recognize them by their way of walking, the color of their hair, the dimple in their chins, or the color of their skin.

One Friday, late in the afternoon, he saw a young girl about twenty-five or thirty years old, with an attractive silhouette and a very feminine and lilting gait. Even though he only saw her from behind, it was enough to recognize her. She wore a black dress tight to her body like the ones Susana wore, high heels, and she was coming from Santa Fe Avenue with a shopping bag from a local boutique. She turned at the corner of Juncal Street on the way to her apartment.

Raúl pointed her out to Alfredo so he could recognize her and got close to her from behind—close enough that she had the feeling she was been followed. That made her worry and speed up her pace. She had only a block and a half to go to reach her apartment and was glad that the streets were full of people. She decided to turn to look back at Alfredo, who was barely two steps away, ready to talk to her. But when she turned around, Raúl realized instantly that she was not his daughter. Fortunately, she did not make a scene but, even though her gestures showed her displeasure, it wasn't enough to attract any attention— which would have embarrassed and infuriated Alfredo.

. . .

Six months later, on a sunny spring morning with brilliant blue sky, from his usual spot in the café, Raúl was convinced he had seen one of his daughters. She had two little ones in hand. She was walking down Alvear Avenue in the direction of the Lady of Pilar Basilica.

Raúl exclaimed to Alfredo, "See that girl with the silk blouse and purple collar scarf with the brown skirt and suede shoes? I'm sure it's my oldest daughter Valeria."

The boy whose hand she was holding was about six or seven years old, and the girl was between four and five. They hardly walked; instead, they were jumping, and they both looked very happy and excited. They were followed by a young gentleman with a blue jacket, khaki pants, well-polished brown loafers, and a light blue shirt with an open collar. There was no doubt that they were together. All of them were smiling.

Raúl's heart, through Alfredo, skipped a beat. There was no doubt in his mind that this was his daughter Valeria. Without realizing it, a tear trickled down his cheek; he was paralyzed and didn't know whether to jump or shout. Seeing the children gave him an amazing feeling of wondering whether they could be his grandchildren. It was difficult to understand that someone like Raúl, who in the past was only interested in himself, who did not make mistakes and was not moved by small things, was so affected today. He was getting old.

Now it was Alfredo who didn't understand what was going on. Many times, in the past there had been a transfer of personalities between him and Raúl. But not today. In spite of that, Alfredo followed them with his eyes until they entered the church. He jumped from his seat at the restaurant without paying for his drink and ran behind them to the church. Raúl's anxiety had spread to Alfredo, who now began to notice a tremor in his legs, a tremor that he had only felt before when he was a teenager going out with a girl for the first time.

The Basilica of the Lady of Pilar was the second oldest church in the city of Buenos Aires. On the outside, its modest appearance didn't reflect its indoor splendor or the richness of its history. It was quite small, painted a simple white, with a bell tower where the white color was interrupted by colorful tiles brought from France. The interior was impressive, with a single nave and two side chapels. The central altar was made of pure silver in a Baroque style and showed a craftsmanship that made it very special. Everyone who visited felt transported to a mystical and historical world.

Twelve o'clock Mass was already beginning; the church was full of families with little ones, everyone knew each other and greeted each other with a smile. The twelve o'clock Mass was the most popular; the parish priest who gave the sermon was an excellent speaker. It was always enjoyable to hear him because his sermons were thoughtful, but more importantly, they were short and to the point.

Alfredo followed the family and sat two rows behind them where he could see them perfectly. Raúl enjoyed every second, but Alfredo complained, "You know I don't like church. The last time I was in a church was for my wedding, and even that was against my will. These people are so hypocritical—when they leave church, they forget every one of the teachings and intentions of Christ."

Raúl replied, "Right now I'm not interested in your opinions. You have to understand—they're my family!"

Raúl didn't know how to get closer without creating suspicion. He wanted to demonstrate some of his characteristic idiosyncrasies, such as scratching his head or rubbing his earlobe, but these would only identify him to his poker companions. He knew that if he actually announced his presence to his daughter, everything would explode like a bubble and that would be his end, as it was with all reincarnated.

Then Raúl began to investigate. Because of the way Valeria and her family talked with other parishioners, it was pretty clear that they were regulars at the twelve-o'clock Mass. He announced to Alfredo, "I know what we are going to do every Sunday at twelve o'clock—every Sunday at noon, we'll be at this Mass in the Pilar Basilica."

The thought didn't make Alfredo very happy.

The next thing they did was to follow them home in order to know where they lived. This was easy because they entered a building only three blocks away from the church, very close to the apartment where Raúl used to live with his family. He wanted to find some way to approach and talk to them, but that would take time. Thousands of ideas sprang up at once; he was happier than he'd been for a long time. But he still had to find Susana and his other daughter, Maria José.

Chapter 14

Ricardo and Virginia had ninety days to fulfill their parents' demands, and it was difficult to comply with all their conditions. Both of them were used to this kind of pressure, since they had grown up in an environment where they were unable to express their feelings or independence.

Their parents would always say, "Don't do this, don't do that," or "God is going to punish you for what you have done," or "Every time you disobey, you make me cry!"

They grew up being made to feel guilty, and their parents had no concern for the consequences of their actions.

Given all these years of brainwashing, their parents never expected this kind of behavior from their own children.

Virginia had already challenged family traditions by looking for a job that would take her away from the routine of housework. Thanks to the recommendation from a neighbor at the Country Club, she was hired as a receptionist in a dental office with five dentists and twenty other employees, including dental assistants, hygienists, and secretaries. Other than two of them who were older, the rest seemed younger than Virginia.

Virginia was very well received at the dental clinic. Her appearance and her easy and friendly smile helped her adjust to the challenges of working outside her home. She was in charge of registering patients and taking them to the dentist as soon as everyone was ready.

The most enjoyable part of her job was lunch. All the employees sat in a room around a large table that accommodated most of the staff. Most brought their lunches and tried to eat healthy, often vegetables and fruit with only a few carbohydrates. Their conversations were animated and entertaining. They talked about their boyfriends and adventures, trips, clothes, cosmetics, and shoes. The talk went from one end of the table to the other so that it was difficult to follow any one conversation.

Pretty soon, they all wanted to know details of Virginia's life. She told them, "I married ten years ago, and I have two daughters at home."

She brought out pictures of her daughters from her wallet and everyone complimented her about them. She also told them that she lived in the Country Club and, to get to the office, she had to drive forty minutes by car. Of course, she didn't mention her affiliation with the religious group.

When they heard that there was a new employee, the five dentists welcomed her. Virginia noticed the youngest of them, who was very handsome and did not wear a wedding ring. The other girls told her that he was new in the office and had just started working right after his graduation from dental school six months ago. He was very kind to the staff, but most importantly, they told her, he was single.

All the staff went out on the first Tuesday of every month to have dinner at a restaurant in the area, and they invited her. One of them lived near the Country Club and offered to share the drive.

Virginia did not know how to explain to Ricardo the importance of these dinners to the group and did not know how to justify attending these meetings. With so many women in the same office, there was always some kind of conflict, but this group got along very well, and she felt anxious to fit in and at the same time excited to do something she had never done in her life.

With ten years of age difference from the majority of the women in the group and perhaps less discipline than in her own family, these conversations were very open and explicit on many topics. The girls showed no shame revealing intimacies that Virginia would never have dared to share. Some of them were more adventurous than others, and often their stories made everyone laugh.

One of them said that one night they had run out of time allowed in the hotel where they were making love and left the room in a rush without time to put on all her clothes and forgetting some of them in the hotel. She talked about how difficult it was to return to her parents' house without being found out, because she might have had only one shoe or forgotten her skirt.

Virginia, worried, asked, "What would have happened if your parents had found out?"

"Oh, I was prepared! I was going to tell them that we had been robbed!"

Eyes wide with surprise, Virginia exclaimed, "I would never have thought of something like that!"

It was interesting the meticulous description they made of each hotel where they had spent only a few hours with their boyfriends. One had a round bed, another had mirrors on the ceiling, and others had relaxing music or flashing lights and sensual perfume.

Virginia mentally took notes of all these conversations and analyzed them. She had always thought she would like to share this kind of adventure with Ricardo. The girls in the office taught her how to wear makeup because they told her it was important for the image she had to show in the office. Using the same excuse, little by little, they adapted her wardrobe. Some of them brought some more modern clothes for her to try, and the change was incredible. Virginia looked in the mirror and liked what she saw; it gave her a new confidence in herself that she had never felt. The young dentist she met the first day began to look at her with interest, and she liked knowing that someone was interested in her.

Despite being busy with her daughters, the house, and now her new job, she tried to find time to arrange the meeting with her parents and in-laws who planned to return to monitor the fulfillment of their demands. She knew that she couldn't accept their conditions, but Ricardo didn't think he was strong enough to reject their proposal. In fact, he was afraid to confront the parents in any way, or to separate from the cult, as that would bring serious consequences—losing their jobs, losing their family, being ignored and even shunned by the community. How would they survive? Surely, they would discover the "double-dipping," and he would be accused of corruption. He was afraid of ruining his life and losing his engineering license.

Virginia tried to lead Ricardo to her way of thinking by being seductive. Her language became sweeter than ever before: "Darling, what time do you think you'll be home from work?" and "What do you want me to cook for dinner?"

When he got home from work, she would be waiting for him provocatively dressed and elegantly perfumed and would kiss him sensually on the mouth.

He liked to go camping, so she organized a family trip for the four of them for the weekend. The idea was to forget everything: family, work, the Country Club, worship. Be together without anyone bothering them.

They left on Friday as soon as he came home from work. She had taken a day off from the office and worked all day to prepare the meals, pack everyone's clothes, the tent, bug spray, the camera, the fishing rods, and the bicycles. It would be an unforgettable weekend.

. . .

After their return, Ricardo took her hand and kissed it. Her plan was working—she needed Ricardo on her side.

At the office, the girls invited her after work to go shopping for sexy lingerie. She saw fancy lacy underwear for the first time, and garments so small that it was hard to imagine how anyone could get into something so tiny.

They were in so many different colors. She chose a thong and a transparent pink camisole. It was a color that went especially well with her skin tone. When she got home, she locked herself in the bathroom and tried on her new underwear. She could not believe what she saw in the mirror, but she liked it. Now she needed to find an occasion to try it on for Ricardo.

That occasion came very soon. She organized the plan for a day when Ricardo had a meeting in the office and then dinner in a restaurant afterward.

Virginia told him, "Don't eat dessert, darling. I'll be waiting for you with your favorite chocolate cake."

He agreed. She thought, *The fish has taken the bait.*

Coming home that night, Ricardo entered the house without making any noise so as not to wake up the girls. The house was lit with candles. He went to the kitchen looking for the cake, but instead he saw that there were scented candles leading to the living room where he could hear sensual music. Upon entering, even in the dim light, he saw Virginia in her new tiny pink lingerie.

She was on the sofa, reclining comfortably on two cushions, looking very much like Goya's "Maja Desnuda" as exhibited in the Del Prado museum, the only difference being that she had shaved her pubic hair and had placed a triangle of chocolate cake to cover that area and two smaller circles of cake to cover her nipples. It was hard to resist such a sight. Ricardo went to devour the cake and then licked at the crumbs until the two of them soon fell off the couch, melting into moans of pleasure lasting nearly an hour, until they were both exhausted.

For the first time in a long time, they slept together peacefully. The next morning, Ricardo didn't even make a comment about the previous night. Virginia was not surprised because he had always been restrained. His personality inhibited him from having a mature and satisfying relationship with her, but she didn't care. She felt that she had planted the seed so that he would be able to side with her in the dispute with the parents.

Norberto, the pécora of Ricardo, was not so sure that Ricardo had understood the message. He explained to Ricardo, "Women are very sensitive. After what she did for you the other night, the mind-blowing lingerie, the ambiance, the cake—and you didn't even do anything for her. You should have brought some flowers or chocolates the next day, or something! If you don't look after her, somebody else will!"

Norberto told Ricardo this without knowing that the new dentist was looking at Virginia with more and more interest.

The approaching visit from their parents was still nagging them at the back of their minds. They knew they would be coming soon and still hadn't prepared a response to their demands.

Chapter 15

Some of the members of the Country Club met regularly once a month at Mike and Anton's house to have dinner with a different themed menu each time. The dinner club was so popular that it easily attracted new members to the group. They enjoyed having a gourmet meal as well as having a lot of fun.

At one of those meetings, the idea of organizing a book club came up. Irene, the teacher, agreed to organize the meetings and, of course, to bring her delicious cookies and some drinks.

She didn't waste any time in sending out a survey with a series of questions about their reading preferences:

- Send a list of favorite books and authors
- Suggest the location and duration of the meetings

The plan was that everyone would read the same book prior to the meeting, and each one would have fifteen minutes to discuss it.

They decided to meet during the winter one Wednesday per month at seven o'clock in the evening for two hours. The first meeting would be held at Mike and Anton's, and Irene chose the first book to read: *The Japanese Lover* by Isabel Allende.

This novel told of the love story between the young Alma and the Japanese gardener Ichimei, and took place in different stages of their lives, from Poland during the Second World War to San Francisco in the present.

The only one who did not attend the first meeting was Felipe. When asked about him, Irene responded evasively.

The book discussion was very interesting; the comments reflected their personalities. Alfredo found the book easy to read and entertaining, but he was struck by the reaction of the characters when they reached the end of their lives, a topic that had never concerned him.

Others who had already read Isabel Allende considered that this book was not up to the level of her other books that she had published in the past. Due to the success of the first meeting, everybody welcomed the idea of getting together even more than once a month. Before they went home, they decided that the next book for discussion would be *Fifty Shades of Gray*.

Irene took advantage of the Teachers' Union social benefits and ordered the books for all members because they had better prices than the bookstore. Everybody complimented her because she was so organized.

The next meeting of the book club took place in Diana's home. Ten members attended, and after the initial greetings and while drinking coffee, they shared common comments:

"How about your winter holidays?"

"Where did you go?"

"How was the weather?"

"How's business?"

"How are your children?"

When they settled down, they noticed that once again Felipe hadn't come.

Diana asked Irene, "What happened to Felipe? Why he didn't come? Is something wrong?"

She pretended not to hear and put her head down and did not respond. Mike and Anton offered to go and get him, but before she answered, they noticed she was crying. They all came up to her and tried to console her. Diana, the hostess, didn't know what to do and got hysterical. She ended up crying along with Irene. Diana finally offered her a tea with special honey that was supposed to heal all one's pains.

They sat Irene down on a sofa and gently arranged her legs on the footstool because her crying had made her breathing shallow and agitated. After the initial silence, the questions began:

"Is Felipe sick?"

"Do you have any problems with your children?"

"Do you have money problems?"

They comforted her:

"Whatever is going on, we're going to help you."

"Let us know when you want to talk to us."

Diana, of course, was still crying herself.

Irene said in a quiet, choked whisper, "It's a sad story, and I do not want to bother you with my problems."

But they insisted, and she summoned up enough strength to talk: "I'm sure it happens to many people, but after a couple of years of being married and having our two children, we went different ways. We found we didn't have anything in common, and we don't do anything together. Maybe the worst thing is that neither of us tried to fix the problem. Probably most of you would think that a separation or divorce would be the best solution, but we don't fight or disagree. It is easy not to fight, because our most important decision is what to eat every night. After dinner, we go to bed together, but there is no physical contact. Our sex life was over a long time ago, and he never complained. It never seemed to bother him. Maybe my obsessiveness interfered with his sexual interests."

She added, "When I was younger, my family repressed everything related to sex, and that still has an influence on me."

But she did not explain the origin of these problems. Everyone listened in silence. She felt better talking to her friends.

"Ten years ago, I started having an extramarital affair and suddenly everything changed."

This stopped everyone in their tracks—you could hear a pin drop.

"I kept it a secret, but maybe twenty days ago, I couldn't stand the guilt of carrying this secret anymore, and I told Felipe about it and confessed everything. He stayed silent and didn't even react while I was talking, and only at the end, he asked me if I was in love with the other man and if I was still seeing him. I told him that I hadn't really felt anything for the other man."

Nobody talked, but their expressions showed surprise.

"What I found strange," Irene said, "is that confessing my affair to Felipe made me feel good, even though I never wanted to cause him any pain."

Irene had been having sex once or twice a week with the school principal—a fat little man with bad breath who always had a sweaty face.

Irene would go to the school early and go directly to his office, where he would be waiting for her with the same plan in mind. Without saying a word, she would throw herself on the desk and pull down her panties. He would open his zipper, and they would roll around for half an hour, being careful not to make any noise.

Some of the teachers wondered what they were doing during that half-hour so early in the morning, but they all knew Irene's devotion to her work. She was conservative and rigid in terms of morality and ethics, and they never suspected that she would be having sex with the principal and cheating on her husband Felipe, who they knew and liked.

Isabel, the pécora of Irene, said, "I know you're just doing this to satisfy your physical needs, but be careful not to hurt Felipe."

For Irene, it was only an empty physical relationship—with no strings attached.

That night, they never even started the book club. Everyone knew that they needed to be more like a support group than just reviewing books. Several of them began to reflect on their own personal problems and wondered if it might be helpful to share them with their friends.

Alfredo thought he would like to discuss how difficult it was for him to have stable relationships, especially now that he had begun to notice a certain decline in his masculinity, and the blue pill wasn't working as well as it used to.

Ricardo and Virginia, Diana and Santiago, Anton and Mike, all felt that it would be helpful to have a counselor to guide them in their discussions. One of the new members had been going to group therapy for many years and considered himself an expert and offered to lead the group. That night, they all agreed to convince Felipe to come to the next meeting, and they would work together to help the couple reconcile.

Mike and Anton congratulated Irene for her bravery and thanked her for sharing something so sensitive with them.

Diana didn't know why she kept on crying, but nobody was paying attention to her and that bothered her. All the attention was focused on Irene.

That night, they all walked her home.

The next day, when she got up, Irene found a beautiful bouquet of white roses on the door with a card that said, "Friends forever." She showed the flowers to Felipe, and although she was still crying, she hadn't felt so good for a long time.

Felipe figured out what had happened that night at the book club and looked at Irene with a tenderness that he hadn't shown for a long time.

Felipe is a good person.

Chapter 16

For two years now, at least once a month, Ricardo had gone to the neighborhood where Norberto and his family had lived. Norberto was obsessed with trying to find out who had had killed him, or who had arranged the killing, and insisted on making those visits. Ricardo didn't know how to avoid it. He simply sat in a cafeteria in front of the train station on a busy, noisy street.

In this neighborhood, everybody knew each other. They walked to the store to get the groceries, and no one was in a hurry, always stopping to talk with the neighbors or to complain about the cost of the groceries, or to gossip about somebody who was sick or had lost their job. But not a word of Norberto's crime.

Over time, everything was forgotten! Whether good or bad—good or bad! —everything was forgotten.

It was difficult to assume that they could solve the case just sitting in a cafe. Norberto insisted that Ricardo ask the waiter if he knew anything. The police investigation had finished over two years ago.

The waiter said, "The police in this place are corrupt. If you want to continue investigating a case, you have to 'throw' money. Everyone thinks it was his wife Norma, except the police, probably because she bribed them with some of the insurance money and gave them her personal services for free."

Week after week, they had the same conversation. The kidnapping had occurred in broad daylight, and there were many witnesses. It had happened so fast that they only remembered two hooded men in a dark blue Japanese car, but no one could agree on a license number.

Norberto's family had hired a lawyer to review the police procedures. He found out that they always followed a routine for this type of crime, and he didn't discover any errors, especially because the police didn't have much to go on. They had very little information from the witnesses and from the autopsy, because the body was found seven days later and was already partly decomposed. The autopsy confirmed that Norberto had died from numerous gunshot wounds, and they recovered ten bullets. There was hardly any part of his body that hadn't been shot. It was not a typical crime scene where it might have been possible to find fingerprints or the weapons themselves.

According to the autopsy, he had been killed two days after the kidnapping, and the body showed signs of torture, fuelling the theory that it had been for revenge. The investigation focused on Norberto's background. They knew about his activities and considered the likelihood that it had been an act of revenge, but since he had recently contracted life insurance, the strongest lead for the police was the beneficiary—in other words, his wife—whose reputation didn't help.

The investigation had lasted two years, after which, according to police rules, if the case is not solved, it becomes inactive.

In the first two years, two uniformed policemen constantly guarded the door of Norma's apartment, and two others in civilian dress remained in the apartment even while she continued to work as a prostitute. Bit by bit, the customers were disappearing, since they didn't feel comfortable being in bed with Norma while a policeman was watching them. Norma ended up running out of clients and start working in a store selling lingerie—which was ironic because she never wore any herself.

She always said, "Underwear is stupid. You take the time to put it on, and then you just have to take it off again when you're ready."

The police considered another theory: that prostitutes sometimes have clients who fall in love with them, and then behave like their slaves, willing to do whatever they ask, even kill. The police followed that trail, but none of her clients seemed suspicious.

They also looked into whether any of Norma's acquaintances had bought weapons, and they reviewed her bank accounts in search of any evidence of unidentified withdrawals that she couldn't explain. They searched her phone calls for the two or three months before and for two years following the crime. They were sure that she had not committed the crime, but they were trying to find a hit man who might be known to the police.

By the time the two years after the crime were over, the police announced to the family that they were closing the investigation. There were, of course, many complaints.

Norberto's father said, "They closed the investigation? If you ask me, they never did anything!"

Norberto's friends organized protests in front of the police station.

One day during their usual visits to the coffee shop in Norberto's neighborhood, and following Norberto's advice, Ricardo suggested to one of Norberto's friends that they should hire a private investigator. They considered several candidates until they decided on a retired police officer with lots of experience.

Raymundo Cortez was a private investigator who had solved many cases in the past. He told them his fees He wasn't cheap, but the family was willing to pay, and they arranged that he would give them a weekly report of his work.

His strategy was very different from the police. He started by interviewing Norma. After much questioning, Cortez was convinced that Norma was innocent, but he was more interested in other information that she might be able to provide.

She gave him the names of friends and family members who she knew were jealous of Norberto or wanted to take over his businesses, and others who had been humiliated by him and might be seeking revenge. She also gave him the name of the drug dealers with whom he had done business and with whom he could have had debts. Cortez looked into the bank accounts of all the people Norma had given him and paid attention to important deposits or withdrawals. He went to places that sold new or used weapons. He didn't find anything suspicious.

In the case of drug traffickers, it was nearly impossible to get much information, since they didn't have bank accounts and didn't need new weapons, but Cortez met with some of his known informants to look for any clue about the weapon. The police wouldn't help at all, and he couldn't find out from them what kind of weapon had been used.

He went to the place where they had found the body and talked to the fisherman who had found it. He walked along the riverbank two kilometers from where the body had appeared, and although it had been two years already, he found clothes that might have belonged to Norberto, with spots that looked like blood. He sent them to a forensic laboratory to analyze the garments, and they confirmed that the blood was indeed from Norberto but didn't find any evidence to help identify the criminals.

Cortez said without any doubt, "This was a job done by professionals."

He had spent two weeks working without rest, and he still had no suspects.

. . .

When neither Cortez nor the family expected it, apparently the police received an anonymous call from a telephone located three hundred kilometers from Norberto's old neighborhood. During the call, there was a lot of background noise, as if the call came from a bar or a public place, and the caller tried to alter his voice. Despite the noise and the raspy voice, it was clear what he said, "I know who killed Norberto."

The caller knew that in order to be believed, he had to give them some information that the police knew but hadn't made public. He said, "There were two of them: one with a 9mm pistol and the other one with a .38 Special. Ciao." Then he hung up.

That information matched the diameters of the bullets found on the body. There was no doubt that the call had been made by someone who knew the criminals. The police expected him to call again. Thanks to this new information, they decided to reopen the case and told Norberto's family, who got excited thinking that they might finally find the murderers.

Norberto was glad to hear the news, but Ricardo thought: *This is never going to end. I have enough problems at home and at work, and we still haven't heard the ultimatum from our parents.*

Ricardo was overwhelmed. He felt like he was sinking deeper and deeper into a bottomless pit.

For a week they had no more news, until finally the police received another call from the same man, but from a different location. They couldn't figure out where he was calling from.

Again, the harsh voice with a lot of background noise. He told them that he had been the one driving the blue

Toyota, that it was stolen, and that now it was painted black. Immediately after the crime, they had painted it, but they had kept the same license plate. The police never found the car, even though it had been abandoned months later very near the police station.

This time, the police were more prepared to ask questions, and said to the caller, "What makes you call us now, two years after the crime?"

"Because the son of a bitch who hired us only paid half the amount we were supposed to get, and we told him that if the money didn't come within two weeks, we were going to call the police."

"Who is it?"

"I'm not going to make it that easy—that's your job. Maybe if you give me the other 50,000 pesos, we could work something out," and he hung up.

Several officers went to Norberto's parents' house to tell them about from this call. They said that the caller was willing to give them the name of the person who had hired them in exchange for the money he hadn't been able to collect.

Friends and family went on a campaign to raise the money. In less than three days, they had collected 50,000 pesos. The only one who was not there to help was Norberto's younger brother, who had moved to Brazil for business. Everyone was waiting for the next call.

Ricardo returned to La Matanza café, and the waiter told him, "It looks like there is fresh news; the police have a new lead. The last time the man called, he asked for 50,000 pesos."

Norberto intruded and said to Ricardo, "Let's go rob a bank!"

The waiter continued, "It seems that between the family, neighbors, and friends, they have already raised all the money. Now they are just waiting for him to call again."

A few days passed until the long-awaited phone call arrived. "Do you have the cash?"

"Yes, but first we want proof that you will tell us what we want to know."

"We already did the work and killed Norberto. Now you have to pay, and stop fucking with me."

He gave them instructions on where to leave the money—a kid from the neighborhood was going to pick it up, and if he saw anyone following the boy, the agreement would be over.

"When I get the money, I'll call you and give you a name."

The police did not want to ruin the arrangement. It hadn't cost them anything, and the case was going to be solved. They followed the instructions exactly, and later that day, they received the call. And this time, he gave them all the information. "The one who ordered us to kill Norberto was his younger brother, and that's why he's in Brazil."

"How do we know it was him?"

"Go to the Banco Provincia branch in La Matanza and ask for the activity on his accounts. You'll find out that on September 27, one month before the crime, he withdrew 50,000 pesos."

All this information was confirmed, and then the search for Norberto's brother began. As soon as Norberto heard the news, he was shocked and disappointed. He had never suspected that his brother might have done something like this. Norberto said, "I wish it had been Norma. In that case, I would have been the one to get the sympathy. But now that I know it was my brother, I feel like an idiot. How did I not see that coming? That son of a bitch didn't respect our code of honor."

Finding out that his brother had arranged his killing in order to get his business depressed him. It was like he had died again. Norberto would never be the same.

Chapter 17

Now that they'd found Raúl's family, Raúl wanted Alfredo to keep on looking to find out more about them. They already had discovered the ritual of attending Sunday Mass at twelve o'clock in the Pilar Basilica, because Valeria and her family always went to that Mass and sat almost always in the same pew. Alfredo tried to sit near, but sometimes they didn't attend, and that made Raúl very upset and disappointed on his way back to the Country Club.

At Raúl's insistence, he asked Alfredo to go once or twice during the week to walk near Valeria's apartment or to sit in the coffee shop, hoping to see them.

Alfredo was upset because, in order to do that, he had to add fifty minutes to his drive back to the Country Club, especially since he was tired after working all day. Alfredo enjoyed life in the Country Club, but he still had to go to the city for business almost every day and would return late whenever he had a meeting—and now he was supposed to look for Valeria, and going to church every Sunday in El Pilar meant a lot of work.

Alfredo thought about renting an apartment near his office for the days when he ended up working late or when he stayed to try to find out more about Raúl's daughters. Raúl convinced him to rent an apartment right in front of the building where Valeria lived on Juncal Street, from where he had a perfect view of the door of her building. His new apartment was a two-bedroom apartment on the third floor, painted a soft gray, very nicely decorated, with a large balcony overlooking Valeria's place.

One of his supermarkets was nearby, and sometimes when he worked at that market, he could return to the new place and sleep there—and entertain some girls whenever he had the opportunity, without having to take them to his house at the Country Club.

From the balcony, Alfredo tried to see if Valeria had a routine: did she go to the supermarket at a specific time of day; when did she take the children to school; how did she spend her weekends? He had to be careful that she didn't notice him so as not to arouse suspicion. Juncal Street was very busy, with kids coming and going from the schools in the area, all in different uniforms, and people shopping or returning home after work. Sometimes there was so much activity that it was difficult to even catch a glimpse of Valeria when she or the children came home or left the apartment.

After living there for a few months, the neighbors began to recognize him, and Alfredo found some women very attractive. He had started to enjoy the idea of having an apartment. He was particularly attracted to a woman who lived in the building right next door to his. She was about thirty years old and walked her puppy every day after work. She was elegant, with brown hair, big green eyes, and a very nice body which she dressed to show off—and of course, Alfredo noticed.

Alfredo watched her in secret. But it didn't take him long to get close to her with the excuse of admiring her dog. "What a pretty little dog. What is her name?"

"Fluffy."

"I bet she's your best friend, because I always see you with her."

"Yes, she's great company, always happy to see me when I come from work."

"I should get a dog. Living alone is depressing," Alfredo said. And he added without wasting any time, "I own several supermarkets that are taking up way too much of my time. And for all this dedication to work, my wife left me."

He had learned how important it was with women to play the victim, and of course, he didn't tell her that his wife found out that he had been cheating with multiple lovers, or that he was very fond of himself, and staying in a relationship with a man like him was very difficult indeed.

"I know what you mean—my husband just left me."

Alfredo looked up with interest and said, "It couldn't be because you're not attractive." He added, "He must be gay."

She started to laugh hysterically.

He felt like he'd scored a point.

"Maybe I should introduce myself. My name is Alfredo. What's your name?"

"Paola."

She told him that she was an executive at a marketing company. She liked her work and spent many long hours there, and especially since her separation, working was helpful because it didn't leave her so much time to think.

"I would love to have you over for dinner. I'm not a good cook, though. Do you know any good restaurants in the area?" she said.

"I know a good coffee shop, if you have the time? Let's have a coffee now and think about dinner after."

...

Raúl's charm was working, and it seemed that she didn't notice the difference in their ages, maybe ten or fifteen years. Soon they had dined together twice and discovered that they had a lot in common: they liked to travel, and they were both interested in theater and classical music. They made plans together for the following months. Alfredo began to feel the same tingling in his chest that he had when he was a teenager starting a new romance.

Their first dinner had been at a restaurant Paola had chosen. They ate and drank and enjoyed each other's company and talked for two hours without a break. The time passed without either realizing it. After paying the bill, they went to her apartment, and before saying goodbye, Alfredo asked to see Fluffy. He had brought a little cookie from the restaurant for the dog, who was excited to see them. The three of them walked around the block, and then said goodbye with just a kiss on the cheek.

Without saying anything, she thought, *How cute, he wanted to see the dog and said goodbye with a kiss and without being pushy! What a gentleman!*

Raúl's plan was working wonders. He was very happy with the relationship with Paola, but he said to Alfredo, "What are you waiting for. Take her to bed! She wants you! If you wait any longer, she'll lose interest!"

The next week, they went to another restaurant and followed the same routine. Despite Raúl's advice, they said goodbye with a kiss on the cheek again and went to their own apartments.

Raúl told him, "I don't know what's wrong with you!"

During those outings, Alfredo and Paola talked for hours. They always had something to talk about. In one of those meetings, she brought up the topic of religion.

"Since my separation I have been thinking a lot about going back to church. I grew up in a Catholic school, and my whole family is very devoted, but with the business of life and work and marriage, I just lost interest and stopped going. But now I feel like I need something more—and I think religion can give that to me. It's something spiritual and difficult to explain."

Alfredo listened to her with surprise; he didn't know what to say. He didn't consider himself religious. Rules were inconvenient. He thought that atheists had greater freedom of thought and could choose their own morality without judgment.

She told him, "Sometimes at night, when I look at the sky full of stars, I feel sure that there must be somebody up there. I feel like that all-powerful God sent us a Messiah called Jesus. Believing and having faith in Him is a constant exercise. It is a divine gift that not everyone possesses."

Alfredo could not tell her that he was only Raúl's vessel, and that Raúl didn't believe in anything or anyone. He believed himself to be the most important person and that he did not need a God.

Knowing that his lack of faith would generate conflict with Paola, he was quick to say, "For me, it is important to be a good person, to help if you can, but I don't feel like I need to belong to a religious group."

Sometimes it was hard to know what was in control of our lives: the heart or the mind. Alfredo responded to the supposedly rational decisions of Raúl's thoughts, while ignoring feelings and emotions that came from his own heart. But in his relationship with Paola, his heart was starting to take control of his decisions. He said to Paola, "Look, I want to try. Let's go to the midday Mass on Sunday in the Pilar Basilica."

He didn't mention that he went to church often because Raúl was interested in attending for other reasons. This issue of religion was not resolved, and Alfredo was sure that Paola would bring it up again. On the days that he didn't see her, he left her some prepared food from his supermarket with the concierge in her building, so that she wouldn't have to cook.

. . .

For their next date on Friday, they arranged tickets for the Opera House, *Teatro Colon*, to the Buenos Aires symphony orchestra concert of Carmen by Georges Bizet. They arrived at the theater separately and planned to meet in the magnificent foyer. There were so many people that it took Alfredo a long time to find her. She'd had a haircut, was wearing makeup like he'd never seen before, and was wearing a tight red dress with a black scarf around her neck and black high heels. When he came up to her, he couldn't resist and said, "My God, you look ten years younger! What are they going to think of me? I look like your father!"

"Alfredo, please, I did it for you because it's been a while since anyone made me feel so good."

They stared at each other for a long time without saying a word. No words were needed.

That night there was no kiss on the cheek. Instead, they went up to Paola's apartment and found themselves in a passionate embrace—soft, like the feeling of velvet.

When they woke up, they were still wrapped in an embrace and smiling happily. Even Fluffy. After breakfast, they decided to spend the day in the house in the Country Club to relax and take in the experience of the previous night.

They returned to the city on Monday morning. They had enjoyed each moment and felt renewed. It was like a new experience for both of them that they had never had before, and they decided that the next weekend, they would return to the Country Club to join in the group's monthly dinner. This month's theme was "Greek night."

They didn't see each other at all that week. Paola traveled away for business, and Alfredo was looking after Fluffy. She called every day with the excuse of wanting to know how things were going for Fluffy. One day, Alfredo told her, "We both miss you very much."

There was a short silence. She replied, "Me, too. I have good news. I am coming back on Friday instead of Saturday. I can't wait to see you!"

Alfredo took Fluffy for a walk every day after he returned from work. It was good for both of them. One of those days, Raúl told Alfredo, "Look, here comes Valeria with her children." They were about the same distance away from the door to her apartment. Alfredo wanted to speed up so Raúl would be able to see them up close, but Fluffy had other plans. There was a tree that attracted her, and she wanted to leave her mark. When Alfredo was finally able to move, Valeria had already disappeared from view.

When Paola returned from her trip, she was welcomed by both Fluffy and Alfredo. They had a peaceful evening and were excited that the next day they would be going to the Country Club.

. . .

Everyone at the dinner was very friendly to Paola and pleased to see that Alfredo had finally found a nice partner. They were all excited to welcome a new friend, especially Virginia, who was sure that they could be buddies. They were of the same age, and it didn't take them long to realize that they could be friends.

On Monday, they returned to the city, and when they said goodbye, Paola told Alfredo, "Now it's my turn. My friends are eager to meet you!" She invited him to the birthday of a friend from high school on Saturday.

That week, they met at the Malba Museum on Friday after work and arranged to have dinner at a restaurant after the museum. The museum had an excellent permanent collection of Latin American art, with paintings and sculptures from the twentieth century, including artists from Mexico and the Caribbean all the way to Argentina. The painting that most impressed them was *Manifestación* by Antonio Berni, a work that reflected the social reality of the workers of the time.

During dinner, and on the way to the apartment, they had more personal conversations. This time, Paola said, "What does our relationship mean to you? What are we together?"

"I don't know what you mean?"

"Well, it's been almost six months since we started dating, and I don't know how I should introduce you to my friends. Are we a couple, or are we neighbors, friends, or secret lovers?"

Alfredo was not prepared for that question. Men in general were less sensitive or less aware of these details. The conversation continued all the way back to the apartment.

"Let me explain," Paola said. "Friends are those who know each other from the school or the neighborhood. They share some things, but they are not emotionally committed. There are also 'friends with benefits,' who take advantage of the physical relationship but have nothing else in common. I don't think that is us. Maybe we are secret lovers, but being lovers implies something almost illegal, something dangerous and without any obligation, and leaves the door open to have several lovers at the same time. That's not what I want."

She concluded, "Do you think we are a couple? That would imply long-term plans, maybe marriage. Or just neighbors who turn to the other when they need a favor, like when you look after Fluffy? In other words, I don't know who we are."

And Alfredo, as a psychologist, asked, "What would you like to be: friends, friends with benefits, neighbors, lovers, or a couple?"

At that moment, she separated from his embrace, stood in front of him on her tiptoes, and said, "I want to be your girlfriend."

And without allowing Alfredo to speak, she embraced and kissed him passionately, without paying attention to the people passing by. They separated and started walking hand in hand without saying a word. They said goodbye with a kiss on the cheek. When they parted ways, she said, "Tomorrow at the birthday party, I'll tell everyone you are my neighbor."

The next morning, Alfredo called her on the phone. "Good morning, Paola. Did you sleep well?"

"I slept like an angel. After I got everything off my mind, I relaxed."

Alfredo replied without hesitation, "I went to bed and turned off the lights, but spent two hours looking at the ceiling, not knowing what to think. After a while, I knew I had to tell you that I'm worried about tonight. I don't want you to introduce me as a neighbor."

Paola felt a lump in her throat, worrying about what was to come next.

"Tonight, I want you to introduce me as your boyfriend." Then he hung up.

In less than five minutes, Alfredo heard someone open the front door of his apartment. It was Paola. By the time she got to the bed, she was already naked. She jumped into his arms, and they made love for two hours.

This time the heart had won over the brain.

Chapter 18

Love is patient, love is kind. It does not envy, it does not boast, it is not proud. It does not dishonor others, it is not self-seeking, it is not easily angered, it keeps no record of wrongs. Love does not delight in evil but rejoices with the truth. It always protects, always trusts, always hopes, always perseveres.
(*Corinthians 13:4*)

After Irene's confession, everyone wondered what would happen the next time they met. Those who had heard her confession wondered how they could help her and Felipe. It must have been difficult for Felipe to face a group of strangers knowing that his wife had been unfaithful. It was such a humiliating situation that nobody expected him to show up.

Alfredo asked the group if he could bring Paola, and of course, no one objected. They had all met her on the night of the Greek dinner and had enjoyed her company. She was mature and had shared the same experience as Felipe when her own husband had cheated on her with her best friend.

Alfredo told Paola everything that had happened at the previous month's book club. Each member had their own opinion about Irene's actions and had questions of their own:

"How can you forgive something like that?"

"How can you forget?"

"Can you start over? It's hard for the one who was betrayed to trust their partner again."

"Do you think they can ever love each other again, or will they just live together out of habit?"

Mike, Anton, Diana, Santiago, Paola, Alfredo, and Virginia were on Irene's side and wanted to help her, but Ricardo, because of his rigid beliefs, was unforgiving. He considered her unfaithfulness a sin which could not be forgiven and wanted her to be banished from the group.

Assuming it would be a long session, Mike and Anton had prepared all kinds of sweets, cakes, snacks, and coffee—with and without caffeine, and regular and herbal teas, liqueurs and, of course, Irene had made her famous cookies.

Irene and Felipe were the last to arrive, and everyone was surprised—they arrived holding hands. They were looking at each other with a sweetness they had never shown before, and Irene seemed radiant. She was wearing makeup, a fancy hairstyle, big earrings, a pink lace blouse, and an especially short skirt.

After the usual greetings, they sat in the living room in a circle. The lights were dimmed, and Mike had lit scented candles. The atmosphere encouraged everyone to share their thoughts. Manuel, the counselor, who had experience in these types of meetings, mentioned that success depended on everyone being honest and willing to share intimate secrets, and of course to respect each other's privacy.

"Let me explain," he said. "When we discuss personal matters, the other participants can offer an opinion, based on their own experience, or can make a suggestion. This can be helpful to anyone who has social, work, or relationship problems."

When he'd used the phrase "work or relationship problems," everyone looked at each other and said, "Who doesn't have problems like that?"

Manuel continued, "Sometimes you feel better when you share your concerns with others and accept their advice because you trust the group and feel supported. It forms a bond with each other, and sometimes that bond is closer than others you have, even with your own family."

Manuel encouraged them to talk and reflect. Irene began to feel that she trusted the group and said, "I have no excuses. I was unfaithful. I walked away from God and my husband. I was selfish about meeting my own needs without thinking about the pain it might cause. Only Felipe's greatness of spirit allows me to be in front of you today, to say how stupid I was, how sorry I am, and how much I thank Felipe for accepting me again."

She continued. "Today I'm here to apologize to Felipe. I'm here to get your help and to let you know that his wife wants to get back together with him."

By now, almost everyone in the group was crying along with Irene and Felipe. When everybody finally regained composure, Mike suggested that they take a short break, have some coffee and try the cakes. They needed it.

When they got back to the session, everyone gave Irene and Felipe their support, and Paola said to her, "I'm going to pray for you and Felipe."

Now it was Felipe's turn, and he took advantage of the dim light and told his own story. "Maybe the explanation for all this goes back to my childhood—I was the slow one in the family. If they asked me to do anything, my brothers would say that I wasn't good for anything. I was rejected by my schoolmates, and that made me feel bad. To avoid being humiliated, I began to isolate myself; I was uncomfortable in a group. That's why I decided to study to be an accountant, working with numbers and with little contact with people. When I met Irene, my world changed. I thought everything was going to improve, but it was my fault that I didn't give myself completely to her. I know that sometimes I paid more attention to my work, and gradually we drifted apart. It's not your fault, my love, that you cheated on me. I disappointed you; it's my fault."

Again, the tears. Everyone noticed that he had said "my love"—Irene more than anyone. She got up and kissed him and took him by the hand, and they stayed like that for the rest of the night.

Manuel took over the meeting again.

"Today we will work on suggestions and exercises to help Felipe and Irene."

The first to speak was Paola. "It's clear that if we're going to solve a problem, the first step is that both partners show that they're willing to change, and that was clear tonight. They both see that they are responsible for part of the problem, and both of them seem to want to forgive each other."

Mike added, "We are so happy for you! We're all going to help you get what you want."

Manuel advised them, "You will need to keep on talking openly about this and continue to discuss the progress you're making, as well as how you can do even better."

Ricardo was apart from the others as always and very quiet. This reconciliation made him think a lot about his own situation. He remembered the night of the chocolate cake, and suddenly, without anyone asking for his opinion, he blurted out, "Do something new, something you have never done before. Do something you both enjoy, like reading the same book, walking hand in hand, or having a picnic in the park."

Irene thanked him. "I promise we're going to do things together that we haven't done for a long time."

Diana was very excited, as was her nature, and she told them, "Promise to hug and kiss every time you see each other."

Manuel interrupted them. "I think we've been very productive, but we have exceeded the time we agreed upon. Let's all go home and think about tonight's experience."

They agreed to meet again in a month. They all said goodbye with kisses, each one of them happy for Irene and Felipe.

Sandra, the pécora of Irene, told her, "That was music to my ears. I'm so proud of you."

Chapter 19

More than three months had passed since Ricardo and Virginia had the encounter with their parents, but they had not yet complied with their demands. They had hoped that their parents might be willing to make some changes to their conditions, but they knew the chances of reaching an agreement were not great.

During those three months, their parents hadn't communicated with them at all, not even showing any interest in the granddaughters. The girls continued to ask about their grandparents, but Ricardo and Virginia told them that they were traveling and would soon return. It seemed very cruel that they made no attempt to contact their granddaughters for such a long time.

On the other hand, it was obvious that Ricardo and Virginia were trying to delay the decision. Virginia didn't want to accept their conditions; she was tired of obeying orders. But Ricardo was procrastinating, and his indecision tormented him. His mind went back and forth, analyzing every detail, and he asked himself: *What would happen if we just stopped seeing them? What would happen to our own relationship if we accept their demands?*

He knew that if he accepted the parents' demands, he would immediately lose Virginia and the girls. Especially now that Virginia had become so independent since working on her own.

Ricardo weighed out the positive aspects of his marriage:

I love my daughters. Having daughters is the best thing that can happen to a man. I couldn't stand to be away from them.

I have a career and could work anywhere without having to depend on my father-in-law. I just need to stop listening to Norberto and his insistence on continuing the "double-dipping."

And he kept thinking, sometimes speaking out loud:

"I'm feeling comfortable in the Country Club, despite feeling different from them. I don't mind the parties or the big get-togethers."

He began to appreciate the changes Virginia had made in herself and couldn't forget the night she waited for him with the chocolate cake.

Then he considered the consequences of separating from the parents and from the cult as well:

If we separate from our religious group, we will not see our parents anymore. Everyone in the cult will despise us and call us sinners. I will lose my job, and it will make it even harder to get another job. It will be like starting over again, as if we had never even existed.

· · ·

That Sunday they went to the Temple. At the end of the service, the parents passed by and didn't even look at them. Even though their granddaughters tried to reach out to them, they went back to their car and left without saying a word, as if they didn't even exist. The pastor knew about the conflict, and the parents had asked him to talk to Ricardo and Virginia on their behalf.

The pastor organized a lunch with Ricardo and Virginia to try to help them find a solution. The pastor's wife took care of preparing the food and made sure she made something that the girls would like. It was a very cordial lunch. After dessert, while having tea, the pastor's wife took the girls away for a while so that they could play without interrupting the conversation.

Ricardo, Virginia, and the pastor went to a windowless room, and the pastor sat down behind his desk. He wanted to show them that he was in control of the situation. He began to speak with a soft tone, trying to set them at ease. He said, "This is very sad. You are beloved children of this church. We've watched you grow up, and it breaks our hearts that you might move away from your parents. They are suffering about this separation, and they asked me to help to bring you back to the church."

He didn't say anything about the parents' interest in reaching common ground; in contrast, he implied that they would only accept them back if they gave in to their demands.

The pastor continued, "Let's talk about religion. Our faith tells us that the only way we can reconcile is to open our hearts. When we practice our religion, our Savior takes care of us, and that fills us with inner peace and makes us better people. Remember, 'the family that prays together stays together.'"

And he continued. "Today we see so many people who don't practice any religion at all and make all kinds of excuses to justify their lack of belief. They are members of a materialistic society."

Virginia interrupted his monologue. "Reverend, with all due respect, Ricardo and I want to continue belonging to the church, but it is the church that has to change, to modernize. You will have noticed the changes in the world that affect us all. We live in a very different world than our parents did, just listen to the music of Michael Jackson or Madonna or go out and see the girls wearing bright colors and miniskirts. You can see the change in the role of women in our society today."

The pastor replied, "The doctrines of the church have survived more than two centuries and will not change just for a new kind of music or a new way of dressing."

Virginia interrupted again. "Still, we need to make changes to attract young people to the church and to keep their interest. If we don't, only old people will stay. I know that leaders like you see the need for a renewal. Without losing respect for the Saviour, of course."

The reverend seemed flattered by Virginia's words, but replied, "There are things that can't be changed, even though social changes are real. Absolute loyalty to the group and acceptance of the rules as they are is essential. Without loyalty, the group will fail. And as the leader of the group, I must follow God's instructions and teachings and make sure that my pack follows them, too. We all know the punishment that awaits us if we separate from the cult, not just physical but worse—emotional punishment. In other words, you can't just choose to follow the parts of the religion that you like and say, 'I want this but not that.' That would be like having a custom-made religion with the excuse of having freedom. That is for atheists. I pray for them. How unfortunate are those who believe in nothing!"

Virginia said, "Reverend, we are not here to make our own religion. We believe in God, but we want to reconsider the rules made by men."

The reverend began to raise his voice. "The rules that we must respect were not written by men. They came to us through the Messiah. They are sacred, and they can't be changed by us."

She countered, "We are not against the divine rules. It's the changes in the society around us that make it difficult for us to continue living in the past. With the social changes we are experiencing, these traditions are outdated and difficult to comply with, and they are going to be even more difficult for our children."

Even more firmly, she added, "I believe that if we adapt, we will be even stronger, and we will attract more parishioners."

Ricardo finally spoke up. "Reverend, we are here because we want to solve a serious problem. In the name of religion, our parents want to control us and everything about our life. Have a look at the list of their demands and tell me what you think."

He gave him a copy to look over, but it seemed as if the pastor had already seen it. Then they began to discuss each of the conditions established by the parents.

Ricardo said, "We have already apologized for what happened the night of the party in the Country Club. Our behavior was deplorable, and we asked for forgiveness. We can only explain it as lack of experience. We had never been exposed to alcohol before. Virginia and I thought it was grape juice. We liked it, and we kept on drinking without suspecting anything, until we lost control. We know the dangers of alcohol, and it scares us. Practically anything is dangerous in excess, whether it's alcohol or food."

Ricardo had added the last part, knowing full well that the pastor had a prominent abdomen and that he ate excessively.

"We only want to be allowed to have a glass of wine from time to time when we are alone in a restaurant celebrating an anniversary. We also promised not to drink when our daughters or parents are present and not to keep alcohol in the house."

The reverend asked, "What is it about alcohol? You can't have fun unless you drink alcohol?"

"It is a good complement for a good meal," Ricardo said.

Look at him! Virginia thought. *I am so proud of Ricardo. He deserves another chocolate cake, this time with cream.*

Ricardo continued. "Of course, Reverend, we want to attend all religious services. If we haven't, it was because of family commitments, especially because of the girls' activities. We have been volunteers in the church for many years, and you know that we offer our services wherever you need help."

The reverend listened to his words with pleasure.

Virginia explained her encounter with the gay couple. "Reverend, if you knew Anton and Mike, even you would find it difficult to reject them. They always want to make others feel good, and they always mean well. 'Judge not lest you be judged.'

"Let me tell you," she continued, looking right into his eyes, "something like ten percent of the population is gay, which means that in your congregation, there are about two hundred homosexuals, and still we accept them all.

"No one in my congregation is homosexual!"

Virginia defiantly responded, "Well, they're hardly going to talk to you about it, are they?"

From the look in his eyes, it was obvious that the pastor couldn't tolerate her comments much longer.

But this didn't stop Virginia, who told him firmly, "In other words, Reverend, we don't want our parents to choose our friends, and we don't want to take our girls out of the school they love. It would be cruel to separate them from their friends. We commit ourselves to provide them with the religious teaching we have received and will participate in all the activities organized by the group that you lead. Besides, sending them to a school downtown means that one of us would have to drive them back and forth, meaning we'll be driving for three hours out of every day."

The leader did not argue, perhaps because this didn't affect him.

"Reverend, I would like to hear from you about whether my parents should choose how I dress. Don't you think it's ridiculous? Did you ever see me dressed indecently? I want to look attractive for my husband without offending anyone. But I will not allow them to choose my wardrobe. How can they forbid me to wear a swimsuit when I go to the Country Club pool with my girls if I have to take care of them when they are in the water?"

The leader didn't want to comment on this issue either, maybe because he agreed with her and didn't want to show it.

Ricardo told him, "Can we talk about finances? I want you to understand that we are very careful with our budget, and we want to contribute our fair share to our church. Our salaries are not enough to let us give twenty-five percent. You must know that to cover all our expenses, Virginia has had to start working outside the house."

Then, without considering the consequences, Ricardo blurted out, "When we donate money, I think we should know how that money is used. But there are never any reports."

It was no surprise that this offended the reverend. Before

answering, he clenched his fist and banged it on the desk. "I will not allow you to doubt my honesty!"

There was a moment of silence. The conversation had come to an end. Ricardo and Virginia still needed him to convince their parents to accept their proposals in order to re-establish their relationship. But now the reverend was angry with them and had decided to end the meeting:

"I can't tell you how your parents will receive your proposal. I don't share many of your ideas. I disagree with drinking alcohol, and with your relationship with homosexuals, and with your refusal to pay your tithe. And besides, a woman's place is in the home. I'll meet with your parents in the next few days, and we'll see what they decide."

And then he left the room.

Ricardo and Virginia were unhappy with how the meeting had gone and didn't think that he would be interested in mediating with the parents in their favor.

Chapter 20

On Saturday, Paola and Alfredo got together in the afternoon before going to the party. Alfredo didn't know where they were going and had never met Paola's friend who was celebrating her birthday.

He asked Paola, "Do we have to bring a gift?"

"No, a long time ago we stopped giving presents. We're too old for that."

"How about just bringing a bottle of wine, or a cake, or flowers?"

"Don't worry. These parties are always very informal, just be prepared to have a good time."

"What should I wear?"

"Just dress casual."

"Are we driving?"

"No, she's just in the building across the street from us. The party starts at eight o'clock so we can cut the cake and blow out the candles before her girls have to go to bed. Let's go. I don't want to be the last to get there."

They crossed the street, rang the buzzer to open the front door, and took the elevator to the eighth floor. Valeria opened the door, surrounded by her daughters.

When Valeria opened the door, Raúl, seeing through Alfredo's eyes, realized that it was his daughter. He was so taken aback that it almost made Alfredo lose his balance. After waiting for such a long time, he was now in front of his daughter and granddaughters, in her own home! Maybe after so much praying, God had fulfilled his dream! Nothing could have prepared him for this moment. All the feelings that one could feel through their whole life came flooding in. In just seconds, he was overwhelmed by feelings of love and joy.

With a smile, Paola told Valeria, "This is Alfredo, my boyfriend."

Alfredo's head was elsewhere, but at least he nodded.

As Paola gave Valeria a hug, she whispered, "Let me fill you in later!"

The apartment was very similar to the one Raúl had lived in with Susana, and Valeria still had most of the furniture and paintings that used to belong to him. For a minute, he felt like he was home again, and he felt a bit of nostalgia for times gone by. But now, he knew that being with his daughter was more important. Now he had to make sure he could develop more permanent ties with Valeria and her family so he could see them again.

Alfredo followed Raúl's wishes. He knew how important this chance meeting was. Many things happened by chance, and this was no exception.

Raúl was desperate to tell her who he was. He wanted to tell Valeria that Alfredo was just the shell that contained him—her father and her daughters' grandfather. He thought about saying something recognizable, things that he used to tell them when they were children, like "If you spit into the wind..."

Facundo, Valeria's husband, greeted Alfredo, and they began to chat. Alfredo noticed that Paola was very popular with her friends and that everyone was happy to see them dating. They were all about the same age as Paola, but it didn't make him uncomfortable. He recognized some of Paola's and Valeria's friends as clients of his supermarkets.

As the night went on, they all continued to drink wine and champagne and eat empanadas.

Half an hour later, another woman arrived with her husband and two children, a three-year-old boy and a baby girl in her arms. Immediately Raúl recognized his other daughter, Maria José.

Raúl felt like he was going to explode. He couldn't share his happiness with anyone!

After greeting Maria José, Alfredo excused himself, saying that he needed some fresh air, and he took Valeria's daughters to the toy room where he sat on the floor and played with them. The girls introduced him to their dolls by name, and they played for more than an hour until Valeria came and said, "It's time for bed!"

Paola and Valeria were happy to see Alfredo playing with the girls. Valeria told Paola how much good it would be if the girls had grandparents in their lives. Alfredo didn't hear the comment—he would not have liked to be called "Grandfather." Facundo's parents lived in Córdoba and visited them only once or twice a year. Her own mother seldom visited either, and her father was dead.

Shortly after, Alfredo told them, "I'm going to the corner store to get some cigarettes."

"I didn't know you smoked!"

"Only on very special occasions."

Alfredo returned half an hour later with cigarettes and Cuban cigars. He had also bought roses for Valeria and gifts for the children. He brought a bottle of scotch to share with the other men at the party.

Valeria's daughters were excited to open the presents. She sighed. "More dolls! Where are we going to put them?"

For Maria José's son, he bought a fire truck. He was very happy with his new toy and went through the rooms banging into everyone. Valeria thanked him for the flowers with a kiss on his cheek that he hadn't expected. He thought then that Raúl probably wouldn't let him wash his face for a week!

Alfredo and Paola joined the rest of the guests in the living room where they told stories and jokes, while they drank and ate. When it was time to cut the cake and blow out the candles, everyone sang, "Happy Birthday," and raised their glasses of champagne.

One by one, the guests were saying goodbye; most of them had small children, and it was time to put them to bed. When Valeria's girls had fallen asleep, Paola and Valeria stayed to talk with Facundo and Valeria. Alfredo thanked them because he felt very comfortable with them, as if they had known each other for a long time.

Raúl from inside told him, "Now we're part of the family."

To celebrate the happy occasion, they drank the scotch until the bottle was empty. Raúl regretted that they hadn't been able to spend any time with Maria José and hoped that he'd see her another time.

When they were finally alone, Paola explained to Valeria the reason for her smile when introducing Alfredo as her boyfriend. "Do you know what happened? I just found out this morning that he thinks of me as a girlfriend, so this is brand new."

Later, when Alfredo spoke about it, he said, "At my age, it's hard to believe this could be happening! I've had other relationships in the past that didn't work out. I didn't want to get too excited. I felt like I wasn't enough for Paola. I asked myself, 'Why is she wasting her time on an old man—she should be looking for someone her own age.'

"Yesterday, Paola asked me if we were friends, boyfriends, lovers, or just neighbors. I didn't know how to answer. We just said goodbye, and I went to bed, turned off the lights, and then I couldn't fall asleep. At my age, I had never had a relationship with someone as fantastic as Paola. I felt like a teenager! I thank God for bringing her my way. Now I have another problem—I don't know how to live without her!"

Paola kissed him on the lips, and her eyes started to tear up a little.

Valeria tried to calm things down a bit. "Maybe you don't know, but we women talk a lot. I've known Paula all my life, and we have no secrets. I knew right away that you were a gentleman, and we noticed the chemistry growing between you. But I have news for you," she said jokingly, "I think you're in this one for life! I congratulate you from the bottom of my heart."

They reminisced about their high school days, the boyfriends they'd had, the times they'd skipped school to go to the movies, the cheat-sheets they'd hidden under their skirts for history tests. There was a lot of laughing. The alcohol helped them relax, and they promised to get back together soon.

The conversation had been a lot of fun, and in order to try to please Raúl, Alfredo looked for an excuse to see them again. He knew that Facundo liked to golf. So, he said, "Paola and I would be very happy to have you for a weekend at our house at the Country Club."

He left Paola in charge of finding a weekend that would work for everyone and extended the invitation to Maria José and her husband Ramiro, who also played golf. The plan was for the men to play golf while the women and children went to the pool.

When they said goodbye, Facundo told Alfredo, "When we play golf, I'll tell you some more stories about Valeria and Maria José that can't be repeated in public." He winked.

. . .

That night, Raúl kept Alfredo awake. So much had happened! Raúl had finally reunited with his daughters, and now he knew of all his grandchildren. It was like winning the lottery. He felt awkward knowing that they were his daughters, but to them he was just Alfredo, Paola's boyfriend. So many things went through Raúl's mind, such as the moment he first saw them on his way to El Pilar Basilica, wondering how he could get close to them. Finally, it had happened in the most unexpected way!

Alfredo was surprised by the changes he felt in Raúl, his pécora. He had gone from being an arrogant, unscrupulous lawyer, in love only with himself, to being excited by the promise of a relationship with his daughters. These were big changes. Alfredo was willing to go along with all of this.

Sometimes it was hard to reconcile one's inner life with actual experiences, and when these two worlds were finally in sync, there was a new happiness and inner peace.

No matter what caused these changes in his personality, Raúl felt comfortable with it.

And finally, he fell asleep

Chapter 21

The time had come that Ricardo and Virginia had to meet with their parents to discuss their demands and make a decision that could have long-lasting consequences. They could hardly sleep. The day of the meeting, they wandered around the house in a daze, unable to think of anything other than how this was going to end up. Either everyone agreed to follow the reverend's recommendations, or maybe the parents might be willing to negotiate. At the worst, they might have to prepare for a complete separation from the cult, and Ricardo was not looking forward to the outcome that this might bring.

Ricardo and Virginia had left the meeting with the pastor with little hope of reconciliation. The pastor's words still resounded in his mind: *"I can't tell you how your parents will receive your proposal. I don't share many of your ideas. I disagree with drinking alcohol, and with your relationship with homosexuals, and with your refusal to pay your tithe. And besides, a woman's place is in the home."*

They had hoped the reverend would understand their concerns and help them with the conversation with their parents. Their parents always obeyed the principles of the cult to the letter and would never disobey the pastor, even when they felt he was wrong.

Ricardo's mother was overweight with a hint of a mustache. She was a woman of few words—dominant and inflexible—and sometimes her actions had a touch of malice.

Ricardo was sure that his mother was going to attack Virginia. She would make Virginia responsible for all the couple's bad decisions. She would say that Virginia was corrupting her son and surely had convinced him to drink alcohol and to let her work outside the home. Ricardo's father—tall and thin—obeyed his wife always, and every time she spoke, he nodded. He dared not disagree with her, especially in subjects related to the cult.

Both parents were worried about their son's emotional state. It seemed like he was always sad. He rarely spoke, couldn't make decisions, and sometimes he was bad-tempered. They thought that it was due to the fact that he was falling away from the cult. He wasn't the Ricardo they remembered—obedient and respectful. Maybe Ricardo's personality had been held back until after he got married. Or maybe the real Ricardo had only appeared after he separated from his parents' daily influence.

Ricardo worked at Virginia's father's construction company. He was worried that after the reverend talked to her father about his encounter with them, he would investigate his performance in the company in more detail.

Virginia's parents thought that when Ricardo and Virginia had gone to live in the Country Club, the two of them had changed and were moving away from the teachings of the group. That's why they believed they needed to recommend such drastic changes. In addition to the six conditions they had imposed, they wanted them to move them out of the Country Club and back to the city, close to them.

Her parents, for their part, had been more tolerant in general and did not want to risk not seeing their granddaughters.

Virginia and Ricardo were hopeful that they would be able to reach an agreement and that her parents would be willing to help them, because they seemed more flexible.

Ricardo and Virginia had spent hours trying to find a solution. They could use the same arguments they had used with the reverend. They considered discussing it with the book club group. They remembered that the previous meeting, focusing on Irene and Felipe, had been very helpful.

In order to confront their parents, they had to work out a strong strategy. It was very important that the two of them stood united, and their views had moved much closer since their meeting with the reverend. Ricardo had shown some willingness to compromise, or as Virginia said, "He started to wake up."

The pressure that Norberto the pécora used to apply to Ricardo had decreased since he had learned that it was Norberto's brother who had ordered his killing. Since he had recognized that he was a victim of such dishonor, he had been depressed. Norberto, too, was changing.

Many times, Ricardo's manners were impulsive and out of control. It had caused him difficulties with interpersonal relationships because he was always angry. Lately, some of these rough edges had smoothed. Virginia treated him gently, using all her charm—frequently presenting him with chocolate cakes, sometimes with cream.

They worried about the consequences of remaining in the cult or separating from it. Staying with the group would mean they would have to accept total control over their lives. On the other hand, leaving would mean losing their families and many other things they cared about. After much debate, surprisingly Ricardo was in favor of separating to regain control of their lives, but he knew the decision to separate, would make him feel empty. He was afraid that it would plunge him into a severe depression.

In other words, if the parents didn't accept their suggestions, he knew that from then on, his family would be limited to just him, Virginia, and their daughters. But then maybe everything would be easier.

Without the rest of the family Ricardo had to start learning to trust and to feel love; this was something new for him. Love to his family was going to give him the strength and the energy to keep on fighting. Love was contagious, and with any luck, it would rub off on his parents.

Every afternoon after work and before dinner, Ricardo, Virginia, and the girls strolled through the streets of the Country Club. The girls rode on their tricycles, and often stopped to talk to the other neighborhood kids, many of whom went to the same school. During these walks, both took the opportunity to work on a plan for the things that they would have to discuss with their parents the following week.

Seeing how much the girls loved playing with their schoolmates, Ricardo and Virginia looked at each other. Without saying a word, they decided that the girls would not change schools, even if their parents insisted.

On one of those walks, they agreed to stop drinking alcohol, although Virginia told Ricardo, "I'll miss having a glass of wine with a good meal."

Ricardo agreed with her but reminded her how bad they had felt the day after Mike and Anton's party. "Remember how we felt like our heads were going to explode? Everything moved around as if we were on a ship!"

"Yes. I remember the next day, when I opened the curtains, I couldn't stand the brightness of the light, and I couldn't even drink water because I was still so sick. And the worst thing was that I didn't remember anything that happened. Do you remember that I asked you where the girls were? Until the bell rang, and your parents were with them."

"And it lasted all day. If I moved too fast, I felt like falling."

"It was horrible! But it doesn't happen with only one glass, and I hope that we learned our lesson."

Another afternoon during their walk, they agreed that having Virginia stay at home was not negotiable. They knew that this should be an easy argument to negotiate with the parents, since there were other women who were members of the cult and also had jobs. Ricardo had already felt the benefits of having Virginia working, which included a supplement to their household salary that helped with the girls' education, all without neglecting the family. He liked the new Virginia.

It was customary for girls who attended the cult's secondary school to learn domestic chores, to better prepare them for their domestic duties and for caring for their husbands and children. They would learn to cook, knit, sew, embroider, and clean—all the tasks expected of a traditional housewife.

Ricardo's parents needed to understand that society was changing. More and more women had jobs outside the home. This was much more common after World War II, when the number of married women with jobs outside the house doubled, allowing them careers of their own.

They also talked about the subject of homosexuality, understanding that it would be more difficult to explain to their parents, and not knowing how to approach it. Maybe they could use the same argument they'd used with the reverend and explain that probably ten percent of the population was gay, and probably many members of the cult were, too, but they were all expected to keep it a secret. Besides, even in the Bible, Jesus never himself condemned homosexuality. The argument against homosexuality was from the Old Testament, and Jesus had said that he had not come to change the word of the prophets.

Ricardo was very nervous. One night, around four in the morning, Virginia woke up to hear Ricardo sobbing. She turned on the lights and said, "What's the matter? Can I help?"

Ricardo confessed, "I had a panic attack."

"Why?"

"I'm afraid something bad is going to happen. I felt like I couldn't breathe, and my heart was pounding."

He was trembling. She hugged him gently and covered him with a blanket. She made tea for him and talked very softly to try to help him relax, reminding him to take slow, deep breaths.

"Everything is going to be all right. Don't worry. We have to be strong, and I am going to be here with you. Think of our beautiful daughters." Her words were very helpful, and he felt better, but he still couldn't get back to sleep. Instead, he went for a walk. A walk was one of the things that could calm him and reduce his anxiety, although, of course, it was just a short-term fix.

. . .

Virginia felt like Ricardo needed to get some help with this but didn't dare to suggest counseling to him. Their parents would strongly disagree with counseling—they didn't believe in psychiatric treatments.

Virginia thought it could have been easier if they had closer friends. This might be the kind of problem they would be able to discuss together. She decided to share her concerns with some of her friends from the Country Club in one of their "therapy" sessions at the book club.

Although Ricardo didn't like to discuss his personal or family matters with strangers, he and Virginia had decided that they would ask for help at the next meeting. They would explain that they were members of a cult group and that they had problems fulfilling their obligations. If they didn't follow their rules, they could lose everything— home, family, their jobs, and much more.

A few days after the initial meeting with the leader, Ricardo's mother called on the phone with her usual rudeness, oblivious to whether they had other commitments. She announced that they wanted to have their meeting on the following Saturday and that the girls couldn't be at the house.

Their book club meeting with their friends at the Country Club was supposed to take place two days before they were to meet with the parents, and they hoped that it would help them find a solution.

Chapter 22

The book club met again at Anton and Mike's home, and as usual, Irene brought out her famous cookies. They always began with coffee or tea while talking about their days, their work, travel, and their children. Then they went to the living room, which was decorated with soft and scented candles, providing a sense of tranquility that facilitated the conversation.

Manuel the "counselor" started the meeting by asking each one of them if they had anything that they wanted to discuss or any news since their last meeting.

Alfredo excitedly told them about his new family. He spoke so much that he had to be stopped so that the rest of them could get a chance to talk. They all congratulated Alfredo and were interested in getting to know his new family. He promised to invite them all to his house to meet them.

After last month's successful session, Felipe and Irene told them what had happened to them since then. They hardly needed to talk; there was almost a halo around them. They never let go of each other's hands and looked at each other constantly. The rest of the group wanted to know how they had worked everything out.

Irene thanked everyone for their help at the last book club, and Felipe said, "We rediscovered each other and remembered so many beautiful things. We start every day with a kiss. We make breakfast together, listen to music, read, and make plans for things we could do to get closer to each other. Irene started to ask me how I felt, and that made me feel appreciated. Every week, we plan a date night, which always turns out to be the highlight of the week. We reserve a table at the restaurant, but make plans to arrive separately and pretend not to know each other. Then we meet at the bar and start with a drink until the table is ready."

Irene added, "Then he takes me to our table, holding me firmly by the waist. I like that. Then he pulls out the chair for me to sit down, just like we used to do when we first started dating. We order dinner, but sometimes we get an appetizer to share, and we always start with our favorite Rioja wine. Felipe always makes me taste his dessert. I never eat dessert because I don't want to get fat. I want to look nice for my 'boyfriend.'" She looked mischievously at Felipe. "When we get home, we sit in the armchair and keep on talking for hours about what we want from each other. We make plans for our future. But last Thursday, after we got back from the restaurant, something was different. Felipe brought me a liqueur, but this time he didn't talk."

The rest looked at them worried, thinking that the honeymoon was over.

She continued. "When he sat down, without any announcement, he leaned over to give me a long kiss, and then started touching me all over. It was just like our first time. It was fantastic, even though there wasn't any penetration."

Then Irene fell into her "teacher" role and added, "There are lots of ways to make love: kisses, affection, hugs, but the best aphrodisiac is love. We went to the bedroom without saying another word, but we both knew that we'd experienced something wonderful, something beautiful."

Everyone congratulated them and said how much they hoped that things would keep going on the same path.

Manuel then looked at Ricardo and Virginia. Virginia said that they had a problem they wanted to talk about.

If the surprise of Irene's infidelity had been something that no one had expected, they certainly weren't prepared to hear Ricardo and Virginia's revelation.

Virginia said, "I need to give you a little background so you can understand. We are members of a cult…"

Upon hearing the word 'cult', Diana shouted, "What are you talking about? Members of a cult!" She said the words as if she didn't believe her ears, repeating with horror, "Members of a cult?"

"Yes, we are members of a cult."

Diana lost it. "I don't want to have anything to do with a cult."

To get rid of any doubt, Virginia replied, "We're not here to recruit new members. It's not like that at all."

Diana continued about her fear of cults. "Remember Jonestown, when the Reverend Jim Jones took his faithful members from a sect in San Francisco to Guyana with the promise that they were moving to paradise, and then he ordered them to drink a juice that contained cyanide. Nine hundred of them died, including three hundred innocent children."

Now sobbing, she cuddled into her husband Santiago's chest.

After a moment of silence, Virginia continued. "I need you to understand that our parents are members of this cult. We went to their school; we got married according to their rules; and we only participated in activities that they allowed. You are the first friends we have outside our group. The day after the party at Mike and Anton's, our problems started when my parents brought the girls home and realized that we had been drinking, which is something that is prohibited by the cult. When they left, they threatened us and said that they would never forget our behavior. A few days later, they returned, all four of them, and came with a list of six mandatory conditions to avoid being expelled from the cult."

She paused but only for a quick moment. "They told us that if we didn't abide by these conditions, the consequences would be catastrophic. We would lose the house, our jobs, and we would never see them again. Please don't think that the problems we're having with the cult started with you. They have been building up for a long time."

Virginia had brought with her several copies of the conditions that the parents had imposed on them, and she distributed them to everyone. They all took a moment to read and looked at each other with a mix of dismay. No one could believe it; they had never seen anything so authoritarian.

Virginia continued. "I'm ashamed to share this with you. We don't know what to do. We went to the leader for advice because some of the conditions don't make sense. He was no help at all. Now our parents are coming back in two days to hear our response, which they probably won't accept, and then that will be the end. We're desperate. They want to control our lives. What should we do?"

One of the conditions was the tithe they had to give to the cult, so Alfredo asked, "How much contribution do you have to make?"

Ricardo spoke for the first time. "They've just raised it to twenty-five percent of our salary—but if we have to pay that much, we won't have enough left for the family."

Santiago, still comforting Diana who hadn't stopped crying, mentioned an article he had read about a group of pastors in the United States who lived in luxurious mansions and who had accumulated millions of dollars in their personal fortunes, thanks to the donations of trusting believers.

"It's a scandal," he said. "And it seems to me that this is exactly the same thing happening here."

"Ricardo and I have no problem with having a religion. We need to believe, and we need a God. But more important than that, we're here because you all have made us think about our own lives, and we love you all very much for that."

Then Manuel took the floor. "It sounds like, one way or another, your lives are going to change, and you're going to have to make a difficult decision."

Ricardo added, "We hope that Virginia's parents will be willing to accept our proposal. They want to support us as a family, and they don't want to lose contact with their granddaughters."

Santiago said that he had read a lot about cults and understood that not all of them were like Jim Jones, but they all shared a common denominator, which is to control the members for the financial benefit of the leaders. They used fear to impose their rules and demanded complete loyalty. These sects based their authority on tougher and less tolerant rules than mainstream religions.

The first to answer was Anton, responding on behalf of Mike and himself. "I want to thank Ricardo and Virginia for the way they tried to defend us, but it is always very difficult to deal with fanatics. Homophobic attacks in society are very common, and they hurt. Every day, there are attacks on homosexuals. Our experience is kind of like what is happening to you. We've been gay since we were born, and we could never share it with anyone. When we were younger, everyone would always ask us if we had a girlfriend, or if we were going to become priests. And you know when they speak to you like that, it's because they suspect something. They say, 'Don't you like girls?' It never stops until the day finally comes when you tell everyone that you're gay. Sometimes your family and friends leave you and don't want to have anything to do with you anymore.

You have to learn to live with your 'chosen family' in the homosexual community. It got worse when we announced that we were getting married. We lost even more of our friends then."

He looked at his partner, who gave him an encouraging smile, and then continued. "After a while, some of our friends who had left began to get closer bit by bit, as if nothing had happened. The most important thing is for you to stay united. In the beginning, it will be difficult, but later, I think you'll find that happiness will return. That's why I think we have to share our experience. I don't know what your parents will decide, but whatever it is, we'll support you both unconditionally."

Diana was crying again. She said she was afraid for the children.

Alfredo didn't know what to say. It occurred to him that he could offer financial help. "Ricardo, don't worry about your job. If you get fired, you can start working for me the very next day. There's always room for an engineer. Buildings always need major structural repairs. And until things settle down, I can take care of the mortgage."

Ricardo and Virginia were overwhelmed by his generosity.

Manuel asked Paola if she had anything to tell Ricardo and Virginia. Nobody knew Paola very well, and they didn't know what to expect from her.

"Of course, I want to say that I'm happy to hear that despite everything, Ricardo and Virginia still want to believe in something. I abandoned my religion for a few years until I realized that I was missing something to be a complete person. God is generous, full of mercy, and only asks me to respect the Ten Commandments. He tells us to 'love one another, as I have loved you.' Jesus died for us. I want them to tell their parents that love should be above all. God is love. They have to realize that rules imposed by man should not separate the family." Looking at Virginia and Ricardo, she said, "I love you both."

Her words touched everyone. They all silently reflected on the strength of love when it is free from fanaticism.

Paola added, "Try to appeal to their hearts before you bring up the conditions of the cult. You have to tell them that the love of the family can't be ignored, and any love that has conditions and expects something in return, like the conditions of the cult, can't be true love."

Irene said, "I want to tell you a few things about love." This was a favorite theme of her pécora, Isabel, who had instilled it in her so that she was now able to share her love with her friends. She took from her wallet a paragraph from the New Testament that she always carried with her since her reconciliation with Felipe, and read aloud: *"Love is patient, love is kind. It does not envy, it does not boast, it is not proud. (1 Corinthians 13: 4-5)."*

And she added, "I'm going to pray for you."

Manuel said the final words. "It is great to hear so many good intentions. This is a very delicate situation, and we are your friends and want the best for you, but you still have to be prepared for the worst. Since we can't know how Ricardo and Virginia will react if they are separated from their families and from the cult, they might need professional help, at least in the beginning."

When they all said goodbye, it was clear to everyone that Virginia was prepared for any outcome, but Ricardo wasn't very confident, even though now Norberto, his *pécora*, insisted, "Tell your parents to go to Hell. Don't let that witch of a mother dominate you like she dominates everyone else around her. Virginia is strong, and you have to go along with her."

Chapter 23

After the birthday at Valeria's house, Alfredo asked Paola to organize a weekend at the Country Club with Valeria, Maria José, and their families. They offered them a night in an apartment in the Country Club guest suites. They offered to take care of the children so that the adults could have a night to themselves. They decided to invite other friends to meet them.

During the preparations, Raúl was unbearable and did not stop giving Alfredo all kind of instructions. He wanted everything to be perfect. Nobody could see what was making Alfredo so anxious, but Paola listened to him with infinite patience and made the necessary arrangements.

One of Raúl's request to Alfredo was to find out more about Susana. Raúl felt sure that she was alive and couldn't understand why her daughters and grandchildren never talked about their mother and grandmother. Maybe she had married someone they didn't like, or maybe she'd moved abroad. Something had happened between her and her daughters. Everything was a mystery, but Raúl suspected that she'd married a lawyer from his old law firm that he knew his daughters hated.

Alfredo was reluctant to ask Raúl's daughters any questions about their mother that might disturb them. He hoped she might come up during a conversation that weekend.

Paola didn't know what had happened to Valeria and Maria José's mother. Even though they were good friends, they never talked about her, almost as though she didn't exist. If she asked them, the answers were always evasive, such as "She's always too busy" or "She never has time for her family," but they never explained where she was or what she did.

Raúl was pleased to have reestablished contact with his daughters. It gave him great pleasure to be reunited with his family. Alfredo also enjoyed the company since he had no family of his own. His parents were dead, and he had no siblings or cousins. There were only a few distant cousins with whom he had little contact. Paola was essentially his only family.

They had put together a plan. On Saturday morning, Paola, Valeria, and Maria José would go to a beauty salon to treat themselves to a manicure, a pedicure, and end with an herbal massage. Alfredo had organized a game of golf with Facundo and Ramiro while the others were at the spa. When they met at the golf course, Facundo and Ramiro found that Alfredo had bought each of them a pass for six months of golfing, which ensured that Raúl would see them regularly.

While everyone else was busy with golfing and the spa, Irene and Felipe took care of the children. They took them to the amusement park they loved. Santiago joined the men on the golf course to complete the foursome.

When everyone returned, they had a light lunch in the garden while the children played and swam in the pool. Alfredo, Valeria, and Maria José sat in the garden while watching the kids. Alfredo learned a lot about Raúl's daughters.

Valeria was the oldest of the two and was a history teacher. Maria José practiced as a paralegal. She had started law school but changed her mind because she wanted a career that would let her have a family. The sisters were very friendly with each other and helped each other out as much as possible. This was out of necessity because after their father Raúl had died and their mother had disappeared from their lives. They'd been essentially left alone and had to help each other to get ahead. Their husbands, Ramiro and Facundo, had already been friends before meeting them.

Valeria's hair was a mix of blond and brunette. She had green eyes, and a striking physique. Maria José was a little bit shorter, with brown hair and lively dark eyes. They both had infectious smiles. While they were sipping their drinks, Raúl was watching at them and was overwhelmed with happiness. He didn't want the moment to end. He was surprised that the girls didn't talk about their mother and couldn't understand what had happened to her. When Alfredo asked them indirectly about Susana, they didn't give him any information as to what had happened to her.

Through them, Raúl learned that his son had left law school and was living in a commune in Southern California, and they rarely heard from him. Alfredo never tired of talking to them, to catch up on all the news for Raúl. Meanwhile, the children came and went from the pool with tireless energy.

Throughout the day, some of their friends from the club passed by their house. Ricardo and Virginia came by with their daughters. After the usual introductions, the kids bonded immediately and played together so well that Ricardo and Virginia decided to bring the girls back again the next day—as a way of distracting themselves while they waited for the feared meeting with their parents.

There was a time when Raúl felt like he was going to finally hear about Susana. While they were talking to each other, Maria José said to Valeria, "Do you remember the last time Mom came to see us? We went to the restaurant at the Parrilla El Ñandú. Isn't that close to here?"

With that comment, Raúl at least knew that Susana was still alive. They never talked about her as if she was with somebody. Maybe she was single? He couldn't find out why she had visited, where she lived, whether she worked, or anything else.

. . .

That night, they all went together to eat at a restaurant near the Country Club, and they invited Felipe and Irene to come with them. Paola had made reservations for a private room so they could talk more easily. The women sat together and talked and laughed. The men boasted about golf as if they were professionals. When the night was over, Alfredo and Paola took the children, and the two couples went to the Country Club guest suites.

Sunday would be a day to relax. After breakfast, they sat around the pool, reading the newspaper, talking, and of course, the kids running around. By noon, Mike, Anton, Diana, Santiago, Irene, and Felipe arrived, but Ricardo and Virginia said they couldn't come.

Alfredo introduced them all as his new family. Diana wanted to make a good impression, as always. She was very enthusiastic and flattering with everyone, guaranteeing her their attention. To be noticed, she was dressed inappropriately for a barbecue, with high heels and a very short skirt, and began to tell them her usual "tragedy" of the day. "You won't believe it, but today I couldn't match my skirt and blouse because the one I wanted to wear was still at the dry cleaners! Can you imagine?"

Her behavior didn't surprise Paola at all. She already knew her. Valeria and Maria José looked at her as if she was crazy and smiled at each other, while Diana continued to talk endlessly.

When they were finally able to escape Diana's monologue, Valeria and Maria José shared stories of their children, their experiences in school and extracurricular activities: piano, ballet, gymnastics, and birthday parties almost every weekend.

Paola and Irene set the table and made the salads while Alfredo took care of the drinks. Diana brought out the dessert and said, "You'll have to forgive me. I've been so busy all week that I couldn't make my specialty, the chocolate cake. I promise I'll bring it next time!"

Facundo and Ramiro were in charge of the barbecue. They both had reputations as barbecue pit masters and did not disappoint. They finally finished lunch around four in the afternoon. Everyone left later than they had planned, even though they knew they would have to work the next day. Nobody wanted to say goodbye. Everyone thanked Paola and Alfredo for their hospitality and promised to get together again.

It had been a very special day for Raúl. Even if his daughters didn't know it, they now had a father, and their children a grandfather. Everyone was very happy. They had shared a wonderful weekend with Alfredo, Paola, and their neighbors. The children were exhausted and fell asleep in the car as soon as they left the Country Club.

Paola and Alfredo were tired but happy. Paola did not understand why Alfredo already wanted to plan to see them again. Raúl wanted to know more about Susana, but he recognized that the weekend with his daughters and grandchildren had been very rewarding. Raúl kept telling Alfredo, "You can't understand what it's like to be with someone you love and be separated by a barrier that does not let you show your emotions. I wanted to tell them that I was their father! I wanted to kiss them and hug them like only a father can. I wanted to do it myself!"

Alfredo had no idea how long he could tolerate this situation, even though he knew that if he told them that he was his father, then he will disappear forever. In spite of that, the more he saw his daughters and grandchildren, the more he felt the urge to tell them who he was. How long he could hold. It was like walking off a cliff.

Chapter 24

Ricardo's mother phoned to announce that they were coming to see them on Sunday afternoon, not asking if they had other plans. She didn't tell them the reason for the visit, although they all knew what it was for.

The time had finally come. Virginia and Ricardo had gone through so much anxiety knowing what was at stake. They didn't know if this was the beginning or the end of a relationship.

To get ready for their parent's visit, Virginia called Irene to ask if she could babysit the girls, as the parents had said that they didn't want the girls around. In any case, Virginia wanted to make sure that the girls didn't hear anything in case there were heated arguments. Paola called to offer support to Irene and help her take care of the girls.

Ricardo and Virginia once again rehearsed their arguments to prepare a better strategy for defending themselves against their parent's religious fanaticism. It seemed to Virginia that the parents were just interested in controlling their lives in the name of religion. She doubted that it was just religious fanaticism; she believed that the parents were more concerned with the other demands than with the true beliefs of the cult.

The original conflict with the parents that started everything had been the party at Mike and Anton's home, but in reality, the conflict had been building for a long time.

Hours before the parents even arrived, they paced from one side of the house to the other, not knowing what to do or say, worrying all the while.

Virginia decided that Ricardo should start the discussion, being the "man of the house." In the last few minutes before the parents arrived, they made a final review of their plan. Following their friends' recommendations, Virginia would emphasize that "family love" was more important than anything else.

Virginia said to Ricardo, "Make sure we don't get angry. We'll stay calm and explain our feelings rationally. We have to look for common ground and try to find the best solution for all of us."

Despite all their good intentions, they knew it was going to be difficult; they had to find a way to honor their demands and still defend the family.

She told Ricardo, "We'll explain our position clearly and simply, and if we have to, remind them that they are also responsible for finding a solution."

The parents arrived in separate cars. That was unusual, and Virginia wondered if it meant that there was disagreement between her parents and Ricardo's. Her parents were the first to arrive, and although they didn't really show much affection, they asked about the girls.

"They're over at a friend's house. They're both so big and beautiful—you should see them! They're always asking for you."

Minutes later, Ricardo's parents arrived. His mother had already gotten out of the car, looking furious and unfriendly, her face betraying her emotions. Without even saying hello, ignoring their greetings, she refused to have tea, and without any hesitation or even consulting her husband or Virginia's parents, she launched into her rant.

They sat together in the dimly lit living room. Virginia and Ricardo sat together on the sofa, and all four parents were at the opposite end, separated from them by a coffee table. The "witch," as Norberto often called Ricardo's mother, was looking very frightening. Her neck veins were swollen as she shook a threatening forefinger at Ricardo and Virginia with the purpose of intimidating them. Nearly shouting, she told them, "We're not here just to visit. We're here to repair the damage you have done to us, and to have you apologize for the disrespectful way you have treated our leader. We will *not* tolerate you trying to manipulate the principles of our religion to suit your liking!"

Ricardo spoke hesitantly. "Thank you for coming to try to solve something that has the risk of affecting family ties forever." He rubbed his hands nervously as he spoke, and a cold sweat began to bead on his forehead. "What separates us are rules that have been written by man. These are sometimes open to interpretation. I want you to know that family comes first."

He watched their eyes fearlessly and said in a firm voice, making sure they understood, "Family comes first," and added, "As our leader said, 'The family that prays together stays together.' Virginia and I made the mistake of drinking too much, and we apologize. We promise that will never happen again."

It seemed as if his mother didn't hear him at all. She continued clenching her teeth in anger.

Norberto the pécora told Ricardo, "The witch is furious! The only way to calm her down is to hit her over the head with a baseball bat! She won't stop until she gets total surrender. She's not here to listen to you guys."

Just then, Virginia's mother opened up in a conciliatory tone. "I think it's good that you promise to never drink again. Alcohol divides families." Her husband nodded his head.

At least they didn't disapprove of going to parties where alcohol would be served. It was enough that they weren't going to drink.

When Virginia spoke, she addressed everyone with a friendly smile. No one could see her internal tremor or sense the lump in her throat. With that same smile, she announced that they would not change the girls to the cult's school. They would continue going to the school near the Country Club.

That announcement provoked screaming from Ricardo's mother. "They are going to keep those sweet angels in the devil's school! The atheists and the unfaithful are going to ruin them!"

With a stronger tone, but without getting angry, Virginia said, "I know that you don't all agree with us, but you need to know that together, all of us, we have to find a solution to this problem. We are a young family. We need to have independence and a life of our own."

This provoked an immediate reaction from Ricardo's mother. She attacked Virginia. "You mean wearing those short skirts? Who do you think you are provoking with those short skirts? Surely, you're trying to attract another man!"

Virginia stared at her, doing her best to stay calm, and answered, "I hope that everyone doesn't share that opinion. I want you to know that the only one I'm trying to be attractive for is your son. Not just in the way I dress. He loves my famous chocolate cake, and I serve it in a very special dish. He devours it and never leaves a crumb."

Of course, Ricardo's mother would be thinking of a very fine porcelain dish. She would never have imagined that the dish Virginia was talking about was her mound of Venus!

Virginia's mother intervened. "I know you want to dress like a young girl, but it's really not appropriate when you go to religious services."

"No problem. I can go to services in more classic clothes and blend in with the rest of the congregation."

Everyone felt the tension. Then Ricardo, in a calm tone, said, "As you can see, we are willing to compromise, but things will be different."

There were still delicate issues left to discuss—namely, their new friends. Virginia opened the topic. "Since we moved to the Country Club, we've met new people, and we've made many friends. Everyone helps each other. We have regular social gatherings. It's been a different and positive experience."

But nothing she said seemed to satisfy them, and Ricardo's father interrupted Virginia. "I could never go to a party where there were homosexuals. Have you ever thought about how much this would confuse your daughters?"

Virginia replied, "Our daughters' education is our responsibility!"

Ricardo's mother said, "We can't accept that you or my granddaughters could have a friendship with homosexuals!"

Virginia's parents nodded. The negotiations were going to fail unless someone made a concession.

On top of that, Ricardo's father argued that they needed to continue to pay their tithe to the cult, even with the recent increase.

This roused Virginia's anger. Almost crying, she said, "If we pay what they ask, we won't be able to afford some essential things for the family. Ricardo only wants to know how the tithe is being spent! We have learned that when the leader goes away unannounced for two weeks, he goes to an oceanfront mansion that he owns in Miami, and when his wife is not there, he brings some of the young girls from the congregation."

Ricardo's mother stood up, furious, and shouted, "You're going to Hell. You are not my family anymore. You are dead to me!" She turned around and left, bringing her husband with her and screaming insults as she went.

Tragically, fanaticism had separated them forever.

Virginia's mother cried in silence. She realized that she had lost a daughter and her granddaughters. She and her husband left without saying another word.

Virginia and Ricardo knew at that moment that they couldn't go back to their families. From now on, they were alone, but in control of their own lives. That was the price of freedom. They stayed in the living room, speechless, sobbing in silence until they both fell asleep.

. . .

The next day when Irene returned with the girls, Ricardo and Virginia looked miserable. They embraced their daughters as if it was a farewell for them, too. Even if they didn't know it, they had also lost their families.

Paola came to help them, and little by little, everyone found out about what had happened and tried to comfort them. It was even worse the next day when Ricardo went back to work and learned that he had been fired from his job. They also received a letter saying that their parents would no longer help with their mortgage. They would have to leave the house in the Country Club. They also received a notice from the pastor that they were excommunicated from the group for life.

Alfredo wasted no time. He went right to Ricardo's house and offered him a contract to work for his company in charge of the supermarket infrastructure, with a salary equivalent to what he had been earning from Virginia's father. When Ricardo arrived at his new job the next day,

Alfredo showed him to his new office, where his secretary was waiting for him.

Raúl, being a lawyer, told Alfredo, "Ricardo should take them to court for dismissal without cause!"

When Alfredo relayed that to him, Ricardo said he didn't want to go to trial. He worried that they would find out about the double-dipping, and he might end up in jail, though he didn't say so, of course.

Santiago and Alfredo went to the bank with Ricardo, met with the bank manager, and took over Ricardo's mortgage for a year. Despite all this help from everyone around him, Ricardo continued to wander through his days like a sleepwalker—he had lost all hope. Without hope, there was no life.

He could manage for now, but he wondered for how long.

Chapter 25

*For we brought nothing into the world, and we
can take nothing out of it. But if we have food and
clothing, we will be content with that.*
(1 Timothy 6:7-8)

Raúl's daughters were organizing a trip to the
countryside, to visit friends who live in an estate
in the province of Buenos Aires, during the Easter
long weekend. They planned to leave on Wednesday, in
order to avoid the expected heavy traffic on the Thursday
morning roads, when everyone else would be leaving the
city for the celebration. Their friend's house was about 500
kilometers from downtown Buenos Aires. They planned
to return on Monday afternoon. The girls invited Paola
and Alfredo to accompany them. He could join Ramiro,
Facundo, and his friend to golf, while the women and
children would go horseback riding, and then have lunch
and enjoy the pool.

Paola and Alfredo eagerly accepted, not knowing about
the trip they had planned on Sunday to a convent near the
estate. This visit was organized so that Raúl's daughters

could go to Mass, but the plan was for everyone to go to the convent, not just the women.

On Wednesday afternoon, when they returned from work and the kids got home from school, they packed their things in the two cars and set out on the road. When it got dark after about 350 kilometers, they stopped to sleep in a hotel with a restaurant on the highway and arranged to have an early breakfast to arrive at the estate around nine o'clock, with enough time to play eighteen holes.

They were so excited to visit the ranch that everyone woke up half an hour early. It was something new for them, and the children wanted to ride the horses, see the animals, and gather the fresh eggs from the chickens.

The friends received them with great joy and hugs. They were new to the country since they had decided to leave the city to manage his father's estate. This was the first time they'd had any visitors since they moved and they had a lot to catch up on about gossip and news from the city.

After the kisses and hugs, the conversations began. Everyone began speaking at once:

"We're so happy you came. We miss you all so much!"

"We also miss you guys! I miss the long walks taking the kids to school."

"I wish we could still go shopping like we did every Thursday after taking the kids to the gym."

Looking at the estate, Valeria said, "This place is fantastic. It's just so beautiful! It must be great to not have to fight the traffic. And the air is so clean; there is no pollution!"

"Yes, it's true, and we're enjoying it a lot, but it's taking time to adjust. Believe me, everything is so different here."

"Everything is so quiet, I think I would love to live here," Maria José said, "and besides, you're only six hours away from the city."

"His parents are happy to have us here. They didn't trust their ranch foreman. He was always calling them to say that some cows had disappeared, but they suspected he had sold them and kept the money."

After Paola introduced Alfredo to her friends—the owners of the house—the men went to the golf club.

It was a sunny, cloudless day, pleasant temperature, perfect for playing golf. On their way, everyone was laughing at Facundo's jokes. He said, "Since the four of us are not very good at playing golf, the most important thing is to have fun and not pay too much attention to the scores. How about if we stop counting as soon as we reach one hundred strokes?"

The women and children found very tame horses to ride and circled the ranch for more than two hours. After a light lunch, which is traditional on farms because they all had a very large breakfast, they all had a relaxing nap. That night, they prepared a traditional Easter dinner together, with Norwegian cod that Alfredo had brought from his supermarket, using a recipe given to him by his mother, with potatoes, chickpeas, and spinach.

While they were preparing dinner, they chatted, laughed and nibbled on olives and cheese, served with good wine or an aperitif. Everyone praised Alfredo's cooking because the cod was exquisite. After the meal, the men left to play poker and drink liquor, while the women put the children to bed. They kept on talking until two in the morning!

At bedtime, Alfredo was surprised that Raúl had been so quiet throughout the day. No doubt he had been enjoying every minute of being surrounded by his family.

· · ·

The plan for Saturday was to go into town where there was a farmer's market on the weekend. The children slept like angels away from the noise of the city, until the roosters announced a new day. Gradually everyone got up, and when they had all finished breakfast, they left for the village.

The stands of the market were arranged around the central square, with local products and homemade foods for sale. Everyone in town was there. For lunch, the men chose burgers and fries and the women had delicious salads. They didn't want to eat too much because they knew that for dinner, they were going to have a very generous barbecue. The weather stayed nice all day, and the kids enjoyed the pool for hours.

At sunset, the preparations for the barbecue began. The first thing to do was to start the fire, which was an adventure for the city boys, and then three local helpers were in charge of barbecuing the meat and sausages on the grill. There was at least twice as much food as they needed for all of them.

Before going to bed, Raúl's daughters explained to them the plan for Sunday. "We always go to the convent to listen to Easter Mass, and then we visit the convent."

. . .

When they went to the bedroom, Alfredo complained to Paola, "You know that church is not my favorite place. The smell of incense makes me gag."

"It's Easter, darling. Do it for me, and besides, it will be good for you. I remember that you used to go to the Pilar Basilica every Sunday."

Obviously, Alfredo couldn't explain why.

On the other hand, Raúl was furious with Alfredo. "You have to do what my daughters say. They are my family!"

The next day, they dressed up nicely for the visit to the convent, which was about twenty kilometers from the house. On the way, Valeria and Maria José told Paola that their mother was a volunteer in the convent and was waiting for them. But Alfredo did not hear this news because he was in the other car, although the surprise would have been especially exciting and unexpected for Raúl.

Everyone was impressed with the building. The convent had been built in 1850, in neo-Gothic style, and was surrounded by endless gardens. The main building was an imposing white stone with a small chapel, and on the side of it was the convent that housed some twenty nuns and volunteers, as well as a shelter for young girls with social problems, single mothers, and drug addicts. The place exuded a feeling of peace and mysticism.

Paola was overwhelmed with the place and said, "This is a little piece of heaven on earth."

They entered the chapel only minutes before the beginning of Mass and had sat at the back. They were the only ones who weren't from the community and attracted some glances. The one who looked at them the most was one of the volunteers dressed in gray, who smiled when she saw them.

When the ceremony ended, they went out into the garden. Susana approached them, and Raúl's daughters told Alfredo, "We want to introduce you to our mom."

Alfredo didn't know what to say, but inside his body, there was an agonizing scream. Raúl was in shock. He looked at her up and down a thousand times and wondered what was left of that elegant and delicate beauty. It was hard for Raúl to contain so much emotion. Alfredo's first words were like a murmur, repeating some words commonly used by Raúl —"Everything always happens for a good reason."

Nobody knew what he meant, except for Susana, who recognized the phrase that Raúl had used so frequently in the past. When she heard it, she looked with surprised at Alfredo.

Susana greeted everyone, kissed her grandchildren, and offered them a visit to the convent. Alfredo felt dizzy and moved with difficulty. His heart was pounding in his chest. He felt hot, and he was short of breath.

Then Alfredo got another surprise. Raúl's daughters had talked with Mother Superior and had organized a picnic in the convent gardens in the shade of the trees. Before lunch, Susana told them, "Every morning, we get up at five, and as soon as we dress, we pray for one hour. Our mission consists of helping single mothers or others with problems like alcohol and drug addiction, through the teachings of Christ. We also prepare them so that they can return to society and have a normal life. I train some of them to work as secretaries, and others learn cooking or take sewing courses so that they can get a job when they leave the convent. In addition to prayer that brings us closer to God, we feel gratified for helping others in need. It brings me a lot of inner peace. We rely on donations to cover the expenses of the convent. They are never enough, but the nuns work miracles with very little money."

Susana guided them on a tour of the convent, the cloister, the chapel, and the dormitories of the nuns and volunteers. The rooms were called cells for good reason. Susana's cell was a very small room with no windows and only enough space for a cot, a closet for her belongings, and a small desk.

The floor was gray stone—clean, but surely very cold in the winter. She also rented a small apartment in a nearby town, but many nights when she finished her tasks very late, she stayed in her cell.

While the rest of the group walked through the gardens, Susana, Paola, and Alfredo stayed behind a bit, and she told them about her decision to become a volunteer. It was a long monologue; surely, she needed to share it with someone.

"After Raúl's death, there was a great emptiness. I felt aimless; my only task was to take care of my children. It was impossible to replace Raúl, who was and will be the only man in my life. I met him in high school, and we were devoted to each other, he satisfied me in all the aspects that can be imagined, and that is not soon forgotten."

Raúl was euphoric, as if in a dream. What Susana said was beautiful and he needed to thank her. He said to Alfredo, "Do you see what kind of man I was?"

Susana continued. "When my daughters married and started their own families, I had very little to do. My friends insisted that I go out with other men for company, to travel, go out to eat, so as not to be alone." She paused for a while—she felt emotional talking about her life with Raul.

Finally, she continued. "But I couldn't. It wasn't me. Single men come with problems of their own, and their only interest is to get you in bed. Some of them have no class. One of them invited me to meet him at a hotel restaurant. He was waiting for me at the bar, ordered a few drinks, and put his wallet full of bills on the counter to impress me, as well as the keys to the hotel room he had already reserved for the two of us. And we still hadn't even met! It was not for me, especially because of the memories I still had of Raúl. Slowly, my Christian faith and the words of Saint Matthew called me away from the materialism that confines us. Then I learned about the work of the nuns of the convent of the Trappist Monastery of Our Lady of the Angels, and I volunteered. Since then, my life has changed; you can't imagine how gratifying it is to help people who never had anything."

She paused again and then, looking at Paola, said, "From what my daughters tell me and what I can see, you have found the right man in Alfredo. He seems like a great guy. He reminds me a lot of Raúl. He even uses some of the phrases that Raúl used to. Take good care of him!"

They joined the rest of the group and Paola called Alfredo aside. "These people do such important work with so little, and we have so much. I want to donate money to the congregation."

Raúl also told Alfredo, "Don't be so tightfisted. Do you think you are going to take it with you to the grave?"

Between the two of them, Raúl and Paola convinced him. When they left, Alfredo spoke with the Mother Superior and told her that he wanted to make a donation and gave her a check. She read the amount and nearly fainted.

Alfredo told her, "Mother, don't worry if this is not enough. I will be sent monthly checks by mail." By now, the nun believed that she was going to collapse; she had never seen so much money at one time.

They said goodbye and left later than they had planned. They were all smiles—the convent residents, the volunteers, and the nuns, and especially the Mother Superior were happy with the visit and invited them to come back soon.

. . .

On the way back to their house, Paola commented, "These days, it's incredible that there are still people like Susana who give up everything to help strangers. This may have been common a hundred years ago, but not anymore."

Raúl was still moved and, more than anything, surprised to find his wife in a convent—something he had never imagined. He thought that maybe it had been good to die, because with the relationship that he and Susana had, they would probably have ended up divorcing like many of their friends.

Ex-spouses are never friendly, and they would have fought constantly. As it was, Susana had kept a good memory of him. His daughters were happy. Susana, in spite of not having the jewelry and makeup that she had in the past, showed a peace and serenity that can only be obtained when one manages to get rid of anxiety and greed. She had stripped herself of all materialism and now radiated a different beauty.

As Raúl would say, *"Everything always happens for a good reason."*

Chapter 26

"The past is dead, and the future does not exist"—
Sartre

After the meeting with their parents, both Ricardo and Virginia were aware that many doors would be closed for them from then on, which made them reflect upon how much they had lost.

The only one who was happy was Norberto, who told Ricardo, "It's the best thing that could happen to you. Now you'll learn to live without those toxic assholes," followed as usual with more swearing about the parents.

The rest of their Country Club friends were astounded by the parents' reactions:

"How can they be so cruel as to abandon their children and grandchildren just like that?"

"How can you do something so mean in the name of the cult? It's hard enough to be separated from your religious group, but it is unimaginable to cut all ties with your family!"

Their friends did their best to help—Irene and Felipe became like grandparents, and Paola became like an older sister to Virginia. Alfredo, with Raúl's help as a lawyer, became like a benevolent uncle, and Mike and Anton were the spiritual advisors. Diana and Santiago took care of their daily needs—a day did not go by without a visit from them.

They all knew what separating from the cult would mean: rejection and disgust from family and former friends. As soon as it became known inside the cult, Ricardo and Virginia started receiving telephone calls during the night, threatening them and warning them of all the tragedies that were in store:

"You're going straight to hell, you traitors!"

Some calls mentioned details about their personal lives, letting them know that they were being watched. One of them said, "You shouldn't let that 'old woman' bring the girls to school. You never know when they might have an accident."

Irene was in charge of taking the girls to and from the school, which was five blocks away from the Country Club. One afternoon, when Irene was walking home with them, two men jumped out of a black car and tried to grab the girls and drag them into the car. Irene's screaming alerted the neighbors and managed to stop it from happening. The car left as quickly as it had arrived.

Once they were back home, they called the police. Diana spoke to the police chief, who was her brother, and asked him to investigate. The neighbors who had seen what happened, had recorded the license of the car. The police were able to determine that it belonged to a cult member. He seemed to have a perfect alibi, because he had many witnesses who said that they had seen him at work at the time of the attempted kidnapping, so nothing could be done.

Irene was left shaking for several days afterward, and the girls were afraid to go back to school. Virginia didn't know what to do. Paola came in to help and suggested, "Don't worry. I will hire a private limo to take them to and from school every day!"

Despite all the threats, they were still worried about losing their old friends. They had grown up in a very closed group that frowned upon making friends with others outside the cult. This separation from the cult had hit Ricardo more than Virginia, but both of them worried about their daughters, who had lost a relationship with their grandparents. When the girls asked about their grandparents, they avoided the answer and told them that they were traveling. Luckily, the children soon grew fond of Irene and Felipe and nearly forgot about their grandparents—or at least they stopped asking about them.

Virginia worried about their own future, too, but she didn't see any way that they could have remained in the cult. She had friends who had separated from the cult in the past, and that helped her with her own transition. They told them that after a while, things would get better. As it was, everything seemed negative, and it was hard to imagine how they could get out of this hole they were in and resume a normal family life. Maybe it would never happen.

Virginia stayed busy with her work, and at home taking care of the daughters. Ricardo was not doing so well: he felt anxious and sad all the time. He felt guilty for the way things had turned out, and although he didn't tell Virginia, he wanted to try to talk to his parents, even though he knew they didn't want to hear from him. When they had left, they'd stated very clearly that from now on, he was dead to them.

Ricardo would ask, "Is there something we could have done differently?"

But Virginia constantly repeated, "The cult wasn't good for us. We must be faithful to our own beliefs and principles. The leader is corrupt. Everyone knows it, even your parents, but they'd rather lose their family than separate from the group. It makes no sense!"

Ricardo had no answer.

She insisted, "I know what happens to our parents. They're afraid to confront the truth because it's socially unacceptable to express any doubts about the leader."

Norberto whispered to Ricardo, "Listen to her. She knows what she's talking about. If they won't accuse the leader, it's their own decision. That doesn't give them the right to condemn you." He came up with a brilliant idea. "Why don't you send a report to the newspapers and tell them about what's going on? Newspapers love that kind of story. Seeing it in the newspaper will embarrass them, and then they'll be the ones who will want to negotiate!"

Ricardo was going in circles. He didn't know who to listen to. Virginia worried because she didn't know how to help him. "Our parents have cut off the relationship with us because they don't want to accept the evidence of fraud in the cult and look stupid."

Since Ricardo and Virginia had been ousted from the cult, they had learned a lot about how to fend for themselves, and they knew that they would have to wait until they could find the best way of fulfilling their need for spirituality in a different religious environment. They still needed God in their lives.

. . .

A few weeks later, Norberto's prediction was beginning to come true. Soon after Virginia and Ricardo had been removed from the cult, they heard from friends that the leader had disappeared without a trace. They heard that he had sold his mansion and disappeared. It became apparent that he had emptied the congregation's bank accounts before he left.

This made Ricardo hopeful that things might begin to change, and he told Virginia, "Now that my parents have lost their leader, there might be an opportunity for us to try to have a relationship again."

Virginia wasn't so confident. It seemed to her that if they had changed their mind, they would already have called them.

Ricardo insisted, "Maybe they're waiting for us to call them? I'm going to call."

But before he could, Ricardo learned that they had already found a new leader, and everything was just the same. He was disappointed that despite the former leader's crimes, his parents hadn't changed their position.

Ricardo isolated himself increasingly from everyone, even Virginia. He was still in grief about separating from his parents. The stress was giving him nightmares, and all this started to affect his relationship with Virginia. He could only find some peace when he went for a walk alone in the morning before everyone else woke up, or sometimes after they had gone to bed. That gave him some time to talk to himself, although his thoughts were increasingly negative. Ricardo kept thinking: *This is all my fault. Virginia and the girls don't deserve this. I don't like to see them suffer. I wish I could disappear.*

And it went on and on.

Nobody understands what's happening to me. They think I should have the strength to change.

It makes me crazy when they tell me what to do! They don't understand. No one understands how much pain I'm in. They think I should just 'Snap out of it!' but I can't. I really can't!

I am frozen. I want to disappear, I don't even have the strength to cry anymore.

Everything seemed hopeless. He was convinced that nothing could be done to fix it. He was overwhelmed with a constant feeling of guilt.

. . .

Norberto, the pécora of Ricardo, couldn't find any consolation either. Every time they went to his old neighborhood, he managed to convince Ricardo to sit in the coffee shop in front of the train station. Norberto insisted that Ricardo talk to people sitting at the other tables, trying to find out if there had been any progress about his murder.

Eventually they learned that his younger brother was still out of the country; some said he was still in Brazil. Even worse, they learned that the police had lost interest in the case since nothing new had come to light after a year of further investigation.

He also found out that his parents had died. First his father, then his mother shortly after. This devastated him. He had nothing left to fight for. He hadn't heard anything about Norma or his daughters for a while.

For the first time, Ricardo and Norberto agreed on something. Nothing motivated them anymore. They had lost everything, even hope.

. . .

Virginia, on the other hand, frequently met with Paola for coffee. One of those afternoons, Virginia told her how difficult it was starting to be, living with Ricardo. Paola told her to keep trying to talk to him, that talking things out would help him. Virginia complained that every time she tried, his answer was always the same. She said, "Every time I try to schedule some time just for us, he says he doesn't feel like it. He spends all day in bed or watching TV. If I ask him what he's watching, he doesn't even know! He sits in front of the television but doesn't even pay attention. Our sex life has pretty much disappeared, and that's hard to take. It's my way of trying to get closer. And besides, I have needs! I don't think he even notices. I don't know what to do. It's either infidelity or abstinence! What do you think I should do?"

It was almost like Paola and Virginia were sisters. There were no secrets between them. Virginia asked Paola, "You've been through that already when your husband left. What did you do?"

Paola replied, "I was single and didn't have to answer to anybody. But you're married. Sometimes you have to forget about your needs and help Ricardo get over this crisis."

That wasn't what Virginia had expected to hear. She had told Paola about the young dentist at work who was flirting with her, and she was hoping that Paola might encourage this fantasy. But Paola kept leading the conversation back to the cult: "This is a special situation. People who are separated from a cult have many sources of help available to them, and you should look for that. I can help. You shouldn't have to take this by yourself, especially since you didn't leave the cult totally by your own decision—they expelled you, and even your own families have shunned you.

Virginia said, "I know some people that this has happened to before. I hope they'll be able to help me."

Talking about her ordeal made her miserable. She started to weep and threw herself into Paola's arms. Paola hugged her gently, softly kissing her hair. They stayed like that, silent for a few minutes.

Then Paola said, "Let's call those friends of yours, the ones who left the cult, and see how they managed to deal with it. And on top of that, I think you need to get some professional help. Believe me, you are not the only ones who've experienced something like this."

Still in her arms, Virginia listened quietly.

"You," Paola continued, "need something to believe in, something to meet your spiritual needs. Why don't you come to church with me this Sunday? It might help you, to pray."

Chapter 27

On the way home after the visit to the convent, Raúl stayed silent, not bothering Alfredo at all. Self-absorbed but, above all, happy. Thinking back, he wondered: *What is life after all? Life is a succession of steps, sometimes forward, sometimes backward, and sometimes going nowhere at all.*

He was very proud of Susana and his daughters and wished he could tell them how happy he was with what he had seen. And why not? It was becoming increasingly difficult for him to keep quiet without letting them know that he was there, even though they didn't see him. Because he was so focused on his family, he left Alfredo alone without bothering him with his own suggestions and opinions.

As soon as they got back to the city, Alfredo arranged a trip to Europe, kind of a honeymoon, without even telling Paola. He planned to propose marriage during the trip. Raúl's daughters helped him choose an engagement ring.

When he told her about the trip, she went crazy with surprise. She had never been to Europe, and since it was a short visit, he had chosen Paris for its beauty and romantic atmosphere, followed by Rome so that Paola could visit the Vatican, especially the Basilica of San Pedro, the main center of the Catholic religion to which she was so devoted.

She told him, "You couldn't have chosen better places. I have always dreamed of visiting Paris and Rome." Right away, she started organizing the agenda of the places she would like to visit each day. In Paris, they would visit the churches of Notre Dame and Sacre Coeur, the Musée D'Orsay and the Louvre, walking along the Champs Élysées and, of course, climbing the Eiffel Tower. In Rome, their priorities were St. Peter's Basilica, the Vatican Museum, and the Sistine Chapel.

Alfredo had made reservations at a Michelin-starred restaurant in Paris, where he planned to give her the ring. He had chosen the Epicure and reserved a table overlooking the gardens. A friend had recommended the Epicure because of its romantic ambiance and fabulous food.

. . .

They arrived in Paris and after a hectic day visiting the city and the museums, they went to dinner. In the restaurant, Paola noticed that Alfredo was acting strange, a little nervous and distracted, almost ignoring her. After the first course, Paola couldn't take it anymore and asked him, "What's going on? Is something bothering you?"

"Well, yes. There is something bothering me," he said, raising his voice.

Paola didn't know what to think. "I don't understand. Is it something I said?"

Alfredo answered quickly, "Yes, what's bothering me is this little box I have in my pocket."

"What are you talking about?"

"This little box has an engagement ring, and I'm excited thinking about asking you to marry me."

He brought out the box and opened it, and without waiting for an answer, he put the ring on her finger. Alfredo's voice and Paola's crying attracted the attention of the whole restaurant. Some people understood the reason for her crying and applauded. As he had previously arranged, the waiter brought out a bottle of the best champagne of the house. Paola was alternating between joy and tears. She hadn't spoken, until finally she said, "Yes! I accept, of course. Now I'm the one who is nervous. You don't know how happy you make me feel."

The rest of the stay in Paris and Rome was indescribable. Paola never left his side. They were ecstatic. Then it occurred to Paola: "This is so nice! Why we don't stay here forever?"

. . .

Raúl began to wake up from his period of silence and became aware of what was happening between Alfredo and Paola. Suddenly conscious of their commitment, he was scared stiff and told Alfredo, "You know I like Paola a lot, and I know that you want to marry her, but the lawyer in me can't help but offer an opinion. Don't you think you need a prenuptial agreement? Because if you separate, and she leaves you and takes everything, you'll end up poor, old, with no one to take care of you."

Alfredo was upset and responded angrily, "What is your problem? You don't trust anybody! You should know that Paola is very sincere, and I trust her completely. I would give her everything I have with pleasure!"

Raúl laughed and added, "You are so naïve! People can change. Half the population is dishonest, and the other half is," he paused for a second, "and the other half is *super* dishonest!"

Alfredo said, "You're such a cynic. I can't believe you think like that! Don't you trust anyone?"

This time, Raúl explained, "We're talking about two different things. I'm glad you trust Paola, but as a lawyer, I know it's better to get things in writing so that there are no misunderstandings in the future."

Alfredo said, "I would be embarrassed to ask Paola to sign a contract. It would be like saying, 'Since I don't trust you, please sign here.' You can't enter into a relationship without trusting the other person. Look at your family. Susana gave up everything to give herself to charity. She didn't have a prenuptial agreement with you, and when you died, she could have had everything, but those material things didn't matter to her."

Raúl was surprised by the strength of Alfredo's response. Little by little, he had to agree that maybe not everyone was dishonest. He let a few minutes pass, then said, "Alfredo, you're right. I've thought a lot about what you said. I recognize that I have a beautiful family, and that is why I want to get closer to them. One of these days, I will let my family know I'm still here. I want to tell them that thanks to them, I'm a changed man, a better person."

He couldn't bear to just sit by and watch what was happening with his family. It was harder and harder not to tell them that he was still there, inside Alfredo, wanting to reach out and give them a kiss and a hug just like every other father can.

He knew what the consequences were for a reincarnated person who announced his identity to his family. He would disappear forever. In spite of that, he wanted them to know how proud he was of what they had done since his death. It felt like approaching a cliff, a point of no return, and it was becoming more and more difficult to restrain himself.

Alfredo tried to calm him down. "You are lucky to see them and be able to participate in their lives."

"That's no consolation. I want them to know that I'm still here."

He wanted to be close to them all the time. He told Alfredo, "Every month, I want you to take the donations to the convent yourself so that I can see Susana."

Alfredo protested. "I don't know if I'll have time to go every month."

Alfredo and Paola's holidays in Europe came to an end. Paola could not take her eyes off the engagement ring and repeated to Alfredo, "It's so beautiful. You have such good taste!"

She didn't know that Alfredo had received help from Raul's daughters in choosing the ring.

· · ·

When they returned home at the Country Club, despite the good news about their engagement, they found Ricardo was still miserable and not doing well. Virginia was very glad that Paola was back. She was the only person she could really confide in. She said to Paola, "We have so much to talk about!"

They arranged to meet the next day after Paola had rested after her journey. Virginia arrived at Paola's at nine in the morning when Paola was still in her pajamas. They sat together on the patio while they drank coffee, with some cookies Irene had sent.

Virginia started, "There's so much we have to talk about. I want you to forgive me for not congratulating you for the engagement. I'm so worried about Ricardo! I don't know what else to do for him. It's really starting to get to me. I can't sleep, and I'm having nightmares. It is Hell! I'm sure that the girls realize that there is something wrong with their father, but they never say anything. When I'm with him, I don't even know what to do, and if I leave the house even for half an hour, I feel like I'm abandoning him."

Paola understood that all she had to do was to listen.

Virginia continued. "I tried to tell his parents about Ricardo, but they told me it was my problem, and they won't talk to me. I cry when I'm alone, but never in front of the girls or Ricardo. I want to pretend that I'm strong. I've even missed some days at work because I just don't have the energy. I try to talk to Ricardo, but he doesn't listen. He spends all day just lying in bed. I'm so worried! Can you help?"

Paola hugged her tightly. Now it was her turn to talk. "We have so little understanding of emotional problems, even though they're so common. I don't think we can solve his problem by ourselves. We need help. Professional help, you know?"

They called Manuel, their friend from the book club, who knew several psychiatrists and arranged to meet with him the following Friday.

Manuel explained, "In times like this, people need all the support they can get from family and friends. We have to be patient. Everyone has to understand that it takes a long time before you can see any improvement. I know that everyone wants to help, but you have to be careful. Depressed people can be very fragile, and any improper advice can set them back for days or even weeks. Let's talk about how best to help someone who's depressed. First, let them know that they're not alone and that you want to help. Try not to say anything like, 'There's always someone worse off than you.' That's the last thing they want to hear!"

He paused while taking a sip of coffee. "Virginia, you have to let him know that he is the most important thing to you and that you understand his difficulties. But don't try to give him any solutions about what you think he should do."

He also explained related symptoms, such as insomnia, bad temper, unusual appetite, and especially that there was a high risk of suicide. Virginia and Paola gasped and asked how they could help prevent something so serious.

"I know that you have the best of intentions, but you must understand this is a real risk. Get rid of everything that someone could use to commit suicide, like drugs, weapons, ropes. Try to stay with him all the time, even though sometimes he will need some space, and you have to respect that. Try to plan activities that he would enjoy. Maybe you could get him to go fishing with Santiago? Mike and Anton could go to a cooking class with Ricardo. These kinds of activities will keep him occupied."

Paola agreed to be in charge of organizing all these activities.

Manuel continued. "I think you're going to need specialized help. I am going to recommend a very experienced psychiatrist who works with a team of psychologists. I imagine that in the beginning, he will also need antidepressant medications."

They thanked Manuel for his contribution. Virginia and Paola went home and told Ricardo that they had arranged for a psychiatrist to come to the house. He accepted without any quarrel.

Chapter 28

Two days later, Ricardo met with the psychiatrist Manuel had recommended. Dr. Raymundo a short, sturdy, fifty-five-year-old man with a harsh but persuasive voice. He made a habit of leaving a long pause between each phrase, forcing the listener to pay extra attention—possibly was natural, or possibly related to his training.

He arrived at the house in the morning when Ricardo was there alone. Although Ricardo had spent the last few days in his pajamas, he made a point of dressing in more suitable clothes. He couldn't manage to shave. After he introduced himself, Ricardo offered Dr. Raymundo a cup of coffee, and they began a consultation that lasted more than two hours.

The psychiatrist explained his plan and his experience with similar situations. He spoke clearly using easy-to-understand language so as not to intimidate Ricardo and, at the same time, to encourage him to open up. He explained his approach, which involved analyzing Ricardo's past, including adolescence and his married life, to try to understand the possible causes of his distress.

Norberto, his pécora, whispered to Ricardo, "I don't understand what he's saying, but it sounds good."

Dr. Raymundo continued. "We have to work together. It's going to take some time, but I hope you will notice an improvement bit by bit—you will need to be patient."

He started asking questions. The first few questions were fairly simple, expecting only an answer of "yes" or "no." After a while, he began asking Ricardo to tell him more about his family.

Ricardo told him that he had come from a family where nearly everyone had some kind of emotional problem. They were always taking tranquilizers.

"How long have you been feeling sad?"

"A year or two, but it has gotten worse in the past six months."

"Do you know what it is that's bothering you?"

"My parents have rejected us and won't see us anymore."

"How do you feel about being separated from your family?"

"I do not know. I'm confused. Maybe it's my fault. It probably is. It's always my fault."

"Maybe we can talk more about that later. For now, why don't you tell me about when you were a boy?"

"It was pretty average, I think. I didn't see my father very much. He was always at work. My mother was in charge of everything."

"How was your relationship with your mother?"

"She took good care of me. She never left me alone. I remember when I asked her if I could sleep over at a friend's house, she said that if I did, maybe when I came back, she wouldn't be there. That she would leave me forever."

"Oh. And how did that response from your mother make you feel?"

"I was scared. I was afraid she would leave forever."

Then Norberto intervened. "Maybe you should tell him the part about you using diapers until you were eight. Your mother is a witch!"

So, Ricardo continued. "Everything seemed normal until I was about fourteen, but my parents belonged to a cult, and like in all cults, the leader controls everything. They decide who you can be friends with. Sometimes they even choose your partner. My marriage was arranged by our parents but with the blessings of the cult."

"Did that bother you?"

"It was the only life I knew. We didn't have any contact with anyone who was not a member of the cult. I was a good boy."

Dr. Raymundo began to dig a little deeper. "Your parents directed your life, and you allowed it. Later, when you started to rebel against that control, is that when the problems began?"

"Yes! And when I tried to show a little bit of independence, they kicked me out of the cult!"

"Have you tried to talk to your parents since then?"

"Yes, but they didn't accept us. That's why I feel so alone. I make life miserable for all those around me. I can't find a way out of this misery. I don't see any future. I've given up hoping that things can change."

"I can see how difficult this is for you. Let's look for alternatives to try to replace what you've lost."

Ricardo got up. He looked at the garden. Turning his back to the psychiatrist, he said, "How can you replace your parents?"

"I didn't mean that you should replace your parents. Maybe we could look for other interests to help you right now, and maybe one day, you might get back together with your parents.

Dr. Raymundo began to see that that Ricardo's problems had a lot to do with his dominant mother. He asked, "How is your relationship with Virginia? Does she usually get along with you?"

Norberto reappeared and said, "Maybe you should tell him the last time you had sex."

Ricardo ignored Norberto and replied to Dr. Raymundo, "I don't know. At this point I feel numb. I don't have any feelings for anyone except maybe for my daughters. I know Virginia is trying to get close to me. She's doing her best." Then, raising his voice, he said, "Why would she want to be with me? I'm the most boring person around. I've neglected her!"

Before ending the session, the doctor told him that he had a very important question. He said, "I want you to be very open about this. Do you ever think about hurting yourself?"

There was a long silence. Ricardo answered, barely audible, "Yes. Many times. I want to die. But I don't have the courage to kill myself."

"It's important that you let me know right away if you feel like you're going to hurt yourself. You can call me at any time, day or night."

The psychiatrist said goodbye until the next session, which was scheduled for two days later. They had talked for more than two hours, and it seemed like Ricardo's first impression had been positive. Before leaving, the doctor spoke with Virginia and Paola, whom Virginia introduced as her sister. He said that things were going to be very difficult for a while, that he would have to schedule sessions three times a week and prescribe an antidepressant.

The treatment was very expensive, but luckily, they had insurance through Alfredo's company, since Ricardo was still listed as an employee.

. . .

Two months passed. It seemed that Ricardo was improving. At least he didn't stay in bed all day.

Virginia said to Paola, "He went for a walk with the girls yesterday and held their hands, and I noticed he had a smile on his face. He hasn't smiled like that for months!"

Norberto hadn't been doing much better than Ricardo. This time, he and Ricardo were on the same page. "I think it's a good idea to see a psychiatrist, because both of us are in the same boat. I hope he can help us. Who wants this kind of life! My parents are gone, and yours are out of the picture. My fucking brother took all my money and lives like a king in Brazil, and it's just the same with the leader of your cult! I am sure he's having a great time, laughing at all his followers.

He kept talking. "And what about Norma? She is doing what she always liked. I was the one who got her off the streets, but now she runs her own brothel! I bet she doesn't even remember that it was me who got her out of the slums." He added, "I have to say, to make things worse, I have to live inside someone like you! Always miserable. There's nothing left that gives you any pleasure. Imagine how it is for me to watch you in the bedroom with your wife—fresh out the bath, white as a virgin, not an ounce of fat, breasts straight out and on the verge of bursting, with nice firm buttocks showing no sign of being a mother of two girls. And you don't show any interest! What's wrong with you? If it was me, I would jump on her! How can you not appreciate that? You know what? Someone else is going to take her from you! I'd be surprised if she doesn't already have someone in the wings."

On and on he went. "I don't know what's wrong with you. Are you from Mars? You are not interested in women, you don't drink, you're not interested in sports, you never smoke a joint, you never go to the casino or the horse races. What do you need to do to get excited or feel any emotion? You told the psychiatrist that you don't have the courage to kill yourself, but that you would like to die. You don't want to die; you're already dead! Dead, dead, dead. If I have to live like that, I want to die, too!"

Ricardo listened to Norberto carefully. A few days later, he said, "Can you help me buy a gun?"

"Are you crazy? Why do you want a gun?"

"For self-defense. Did you hear that they tried to kidnap the girls, and people come to the back of the house at night with masks, banging on the windows and trying to scare us? The cult sends them!"

"If you want the gun for that, then I think that's a good idea. You shoot for the legs, and they won't come back. Okay, I'll help you. Go to my old neighborhood, go to the coffee shop, and ask the waiter to put you in touch with Juan 'the Surgeon'—he'll get you what you need. There are stolen weapons, and he sells them at a fair price."

When Ricardo arrived at the coffee shop and talked to the waiter, within half an hour, a strange guy arrived. He was one of those people that you don't want to meet in the middle of the night in a dark street. He came on a bicycle. Ricardo saw him talking to the waiter, who pointed to his table. The newcomer approached, and out of nowhere asked, "Who do you want to kill?"

Before he got even more aggressive, Ricardo countered, "Norberto told me about you. We were very good friends, and he always talked to me about you. He told me that when I needed a gun, the best was Juan 'the Surgeon'. He could get me what I wanted."

"Why do you want it?" the Surgeon asked him.

"To scare the neighbors who get into the back of the house at night trying to terrify my daughters. I just want to shoot their legs."

"I have something just for that, a 38mm. They call it the 'ladies' revolver' because it's just the right size, and you can hide it in your pocket. The revolver and the bullets will cost you fifteen hundred pesos. In the store, it is four times that."

"When can you get it?"

"If you have the money now, I can get it for you in half an hour."

Half an hour later, Ricardo laid his hands on his first gun. The two of them went to the bathroom of the coffee shop, and Juan showed him how to load it and use it.

. . .

A few days later, on a day just like any other day, Virginia went to work, and the girls went to school. Ricardo had already made his decision. He would drive the car, going nowhere, with no schedule, not having to explain to anyone where he was going.

Finally, he felt free, very free. He even felt happy. He drove without stopping, driving until he almost ran out of gas. He had already crossed the border, leaving Buenos Aires. Before entering Córdoba, he stopped and filled the tank with gas, bought a sandwich, and got back on the road. Without even realizing it, he reached the foothills of the Córdoba Mountains, a place where he had spent many summers with his family.

Everything was just like it was the last time he had seen it. The same dirt roads that took him to the lake where he met friends and went swimming. The same dirt roads that took him to ride horses in the afternoons. So many memories! It was the last time he had really been happy. The innocence of childhood.

. . .

That afternoon, when Virginia returned from work, she found a white envelope on the kitchen table with her name written on it in Ricardo's handwriting. When she opened it, she read

> *Dear Virginia,*
>
> *I'm sorry. I can't stand the pain anymore. I have decided to end my life. It's the only thing I can do to free you from this misery I have caused. I am sorry for the pain that I will cause those who are left, but I can't live like this. I can't keep pretending. I know you are strong, and with the girls, you will find happiness that I can't give you any more.*
> *I hope to see you in the next life.*
> *I love you,*
> *Ricardo*

She could barely hold the letter, her hands were trembling so much. She could hardly read the words through her tears. She almost fainted, but she had the strength to run out to look for Paola. When she found her, Virginia was pale and speechless, just showing her the letter. Paola didn't know what to say or do. She hugged her and tried to comfort her. With a very soft voice, she said, "You know you're not alone. We'll get through this together."

. . .

Even as Virginia was reading the letter, Ricardo was driving slowly along a deserted dirt road. He drove the car into the woods, where no one could see him. He took the revolver out of the glove compartment. He looked up through the window into the evening sky and mumbled a few words to himself, taking the revolver in his hand and aiming it at his temple.

Norberto was angry and said, "You lied to me!"

"You made me realize that it didn't make sense to keep on living the way I was living."

Norberto knew that he had to act fast. "Ricardo, listen to me! While there is life, there is hope. Give me time, and I will teach you to live well, to enjoy life. If you have a good time, I'm going to enjoy myself, too!"

Ricardo didn't listen to him. He wanted to say that he didn't know how to change or how to enjoy life. God knows he'd tried!

Norberto shouted at him in desperation, "Don't do it!"

But it was too late. The shot killed Ricardo immediately. The revolver fell to the floor, and a trickle of blood stained the seat.

For those who have been reincarnated and don't die of natural causes, they evaporate like a gas. That was the end of Norberto. No one would ever know about him. Not even the worms would find him.

Ricardo's body was found later on that day. Due to the circumstances of his death nobody thought to have a formal funeral.

When the Country Club friends found out, they all went to Paola's house to see how they could help Virginia.

The girls had only been told that their dad had gone on a long trip. Santiago picked up the phone to tell Ricardo's parents. His mother answered, and Santiago said, "I'm calling to tell you about your son. He left a letter saying he's going to kill himself, and they've found his body in the mountains of Córdoba."

His mother replied, "It doesn't matter. For us, he was already dead a long time ago," and hung up.

When Santiago hung up the phone, he sat down, bending his head to look at the floor, and even without saying a word, everyone in the room knew that something was wrong.

Virginia was out of earshot. He told them what the mother had said. No one could believe that a mother could be so cold and not react to news about the death of her son.

Diana couldn't stop crying but managed to say a few words. "I told them it was because of the cult; they are fanatics! I told them what had happened to the followers of Jimmy Jones in Guyana! I'm worried about the girls not having a father, or even grandparents! I'm going to try to give them all they need, just like I'm their aunt. I'm going to spoil them," and still crying, "I love them so much!"

Mike and Anton felt very badly. They also cried but in silence. They decided to organize a tribute to Ricardo's memory. It would be something very private at Alfredo and Paola's house. In addition to the close friends from the Country Club, Mike and Anton included other neighbors who knew them, some of Ricardo's friends from the office, and other former members of the cult.

At the memorial, many brought flowers, and everyone embraced Virginia tenderly.

Paola gave a touching eulogy. She said that Ricardo had killed himself out of love, love for Virginia and his daughters, because he felt he had not been able to keep them happy.

She also talked about the monster of depression that affects so many people and the ignorance of the society about those who are depressed. She reflected on Ricardo's last hours and the mental torture he must have endured thinking about Virginia and his daughters. Finally looking at Virginia, she said, "I can't imagine the sadness that you must be feeling at this moment, but I know that you are going to come out of this tragic period of your life, because you are very strong and you know that you're not alone. Your new sister will always be with you."

When Paola finished the eulogy, it was not just Diana crying this time. Practically everyone accompanied her.

In their minds, many thought about Ricardo's final hours and his mental torture as he prepared to follow through on his painful decision. Everyone agreed that Ricardo had been an excellent husband and father. Undoubtedly for Virginia and the girls, it would be very difficult to get over his death, especially the guilt that would inevitably fall on Virginia.

Virginia's parents never relented and completely ignored Ricardo's death. They never called her or their granddaughters.

Chapter 29

A few weeks after Ricardo's death, people in the Country Club were still talking about his suicide. Everyone had questions that couldn't be answered, as was always the case with a suicide. People said:

"Why did he do it?"

"How sad!"

"What will happen to the family now?"

"I don't understand. They were such nice people!"

Those who knew that he had left a letter thought that maybe he had explained his reasons.

Virginia didn't know where to start. She didn't have the energy or the strength to do anything. Irene or Paola often stayed with her overnight to keep her company. Everyone tried their best to help, but Paola was her rock.

It wasn't unusual for Paola to say, "Don't worry about crying. It's normal. It's part of the healing process. You will feel better after a while. God is your best guide. He will lead you to the right path. Life goes on for everyone, and also for you. This is only a step along the way. It's not the end."

She kept repeating that Virginia should not feel guilty. She kept insisting that it wasn't her fault. "You did everything you could to help him. In the end, it was his decision, and you have to accept that sometimes those decisions can't be changed.

Virginia asked her, "Can I ever I have my life back and be able to smile and be happy? All I feel now is sadness and anger. Anguish. I'm afraid of being alone."

"You just have to look after yourself and your daughters. Look into the future and leave the past behind. We shouldn't judge people who kill themselves. Only God can know what they were feeling, how they lost the will to live."

For her part, Paola's life with Alfredo was calm, full of romance and understanding. Indeed, they had to be careful to try not to show too much happiness in front of Virginia.

. . .

A few weeks after Ricardo's death, Virginia felt able to go back to work. One day, she asked Paola if she could take care of the girls after work because the young dentist had invited her for a coffee after work.

Paola smiled and said, "That boy didn't wait too long to ask you out!"

She replied, "He just said that he wanted to have a quick bite, just to talk about how I'm doing after Ricardo's death," and with a mischievous smile, she added, "You are a nasty person. Why do you have such a dirty mind?"

Paola said, "On the contrary. I'm thinking about what's best for you. I know you've had fantasies about him. You told me!"

Of course, Paola was waiting for Virginia at the front door of the house to talk to her as soon as she got back and get all the gossip.

As soon as she entered, Virginia said, "I'm a very happy woman!"

"I'm glad! Tell me everything!"

"You are such a busybody!" Virginia said, laughing.

"Swear that you'll tell me everything!"

"Maybe." Then Virginia began. "He just asked me about my life, and I told him everything from the beginning: my participation in the cult, how my marriage was arranged by our parents, my relationship with Ricardo, how the girls are coping with the death of their father. He wanted to know about everything in a way that made me feel really comfortable. I also told him that I had left the cult and that's why my parents had abandoned me. And I told him that God had granted me a new sister, whom I love more than anybody!"

She hugged Paola. They stayed locked in an embrace for many minutes without speaking.

"I hope I didn't scare him with the stories of my life, stories about the cult and all the difficulties of being a single mother after Ricardo's death. Who would want to be with someone like me? I bet this is the last time he'll want to be with me. No more invitations!"

"How did you say goodbye?" Paola asked with a naughty smirk.

"That's for me to know and you to find out!"

"Come on, don't be coy with me. I am your favorite sister," she said, knowing that Virginia didn't have any sisters of her own.

Virginia waited for a minute and said, "He stopped the car and looked into my eyes for a long time. I was nervous. I didn't know what was going to happen! But then he put his arm around my shoulders and pulled me toward him. He gave me a very soft kiss on the lips and ran his hand tenderly down my cheek. When I got out of the car, I was shaking! I'm so happy, but I don't know if I should feel guilty."

"Don't be silly. I'm happy for you!"

That night, Virginia slept better than she had for months. For the first time in her life, she had been with a man other than Ricardo, and everything had gone very well, even though she'd been very anxious before going on the date.

. . .

Life for Virginia continued with some ups and downs. One day Santiago, who was taking care of her finances, advised her to sell the house because she didn't have enough to pay the mortgage. She didn't qualify for life insurance benefits on Ricardo because it didn't cover death by suicide. She had a hard time accepting that advice, since all her friends were in the Country Club.

What Virginia didn't anticipate was Irene and Felipe's reaction. They had become so fond of the girls that when they found out she had to sell the house, they couldn't bear to think of them leaving. They offered for Virginia to move in with them.

Virginia closed her eyes and after a long sigh said, "Thank you. I accept. The girls and I are very comfortable to be able to live with you. Already at home they talk about Grandma Irene and Grandpa Felipe."

The girls beamed when they heard the news.

The dinners at Anton and Mike's had been canceled for a while after Ricardo's death, but they felt they had to try to get things back to normal, and when they told Virginia about the idea of getting together again, she was much in favor.

"What a great idea! There has been so much suffering. We need to celebrate Alfredo and Paola's engagement. They offered their house to celebrate Christmas and New Year's, or maybe we should have two parties instead of one. We still have a lot of time to get ready, almost two months before the end of the year."

. . .

Meanwhile, Raúl did everything he could to keep up with the lives of his daughters. With monthly visits to the convent, when Alfredo delivered the checks, he could also keep up with Susana, despite Alfredo's complaints that he could have mailed the checks. Even Paola couldn't understand why he had to deliver the checks in person.

"I don't understand why you have to go every month and drive a thousand kilometers on the weekend when we're supposed to be taking it easy. You could just as easily send it by mail."

Alfredo, following Raul's instructions, replied, "It's easy to send the check by mail, but it has more value if you can put it right in their hands!"

Raúl insisted, "It was wonderful to learn about Susana's new life. Seeing her fills, me with pride."

On the first visit, Raúl had told Alfredo to ask for Susana. That was his excuse to see her. The Mother Superior received him with open arms and blessings. After handing her the check, Alfredo told her, "Could I see Susana? I brought her a gift from her daughters."

While they were having tea and cakes, Susana arrived, looking very neat, her classic beauty now more evident without makeup.

Raúl couldn't take his eyes off her. He gave her the gift, and Susana said, "I spoke with the Mother Superior, and she thought it was a good idea for me to spend Christmas and New Year's with my family. My daughters told me that the festivities will be at your house, and I hope to see you then."

This news was music to Raúl's ears, and he immediately began giving instructions to Alfredo about organizing the party. First, he laid out a list of guests, of course including his daughters and their husbands, the grandchildren, and Susana. Alfredo realized that he and Paola were going to have a lot of work to fulfill Raúl's wishes.

A few weeks before the end-of-the-year parties, they went as usual to take the monthly donations to the convent, Alfredo complaining all the way about having to drive ten hours to get there. Even worse was when he asked to see Susana, and the Mother Superior told him that she wasn't there because one of her chores was to visit the women who had previously lived in the convent and now lived on their own in the city. She had gone to check that they were still doing well and offer them help if necessary.

The return trip was frustrating for everybody. Alfredo complained because he could have sent the check by mail, and Raúl was upset because he hadn't seen Susana and would have to wait until Christmas. Neither Raul or Alfredo said a single word for the whole journey back home.

Even with these inconveniences, no one was happier than Raúl, because once again his family would be reunited. Raúl thought it was going to be a perfect party.

Raul said to Alfredo, "Why don't you and Paola get married that same day? We could bring a priest to the Country Club to officiate the ceremony."

Mike and Anton were excited about the party, too, and started helping with the preparations.

"We'll order the food from our favorite caterer, and at twelve o'clock midnight, we'll have fireworks and music."

Raúl was relentless in his demands. "I want this, I want that, I want this, I want that," and on and on he went.

Alfredo finally exploded. "You're driving me crazy. Why are you making such a fuss? It's just another New Year's, and there's still a month to go!"

Raúl persisted with his idea of letting his family know that he was still there, under Alfredo's shell. That worried Alfredo, but Raúl didn't give up, and insisted, "You don't understand; let me explain. Observing the lives of people without being seen can be exciting—that's the way it is for me—I can observe my family, but I can't be seen. But it's more exciting when you can tell them afterward that you've seen them doing this or that. If they don't know you're there, it's not worth it."

Alfredo tried to calm him down. "But you know, if you let them know who you are, you'll disappear, you'll evaporate."

Raul didn't listen to him. He knew the only way to make an impact on Susana and his daughters was to let them know where he was. For someone like him, this was all-important to satisfy his ego.

"I want them to know that I am their father, that I am proud of them, and most of all, I want to embrace them. You don't know what it means for a father to hug his children."

As the celebrations approached, Raul's anxiety increased.

. . .

On the morning of the 31st of December, the sun was brilliant. An ideal temperature to be outdoors. The party had no specific start or end time. Guests began to arrive soon after lunch; first was Raúl's daughters and their husbands and their children. They brought Susana with them. Soon after, all the Country Club friends arrived, including Virginia and her girls. This was her first New Year's without Ricardo.

Everyone was talking, and most of them already knew each other. Except for Susana. The children went to the pool, and the adults didn't hear from them for hours—only their shouts of joy.

Everyone was eating and drinking. Following Raul's instructions to Alfredo, he stayed close to Susana and his daughters. Raúl asked Alfredo to repeat some of his distinctive phrases and gestures so that his family would recognize that he was there. Every time he was close to Susana, Valeria, or María José, even when it didn't make any sense, he said, "Never spit into the wind," or, "Everything always happens for a good reason."

The girls looked at Alfredo and didn't understand why he would say these things. Others thought it was only a joke. Except for Susana, who thought, *It's as if he wants to tell me something. I remember Raúl saying the same thing*, tilting her head in suspicion.

Susana approached Virginia. She had learned from Paola about the tragedy of her husband's suicide.

"Hi, Virginia. I'm the mother of Valeria and María José, and I know Paola. I know that you are very good friends. You have two beautiful daughters. They look very happy."

Virginia understood that Susana knew her problems and had no concerns sharing the details of her life. "I'm very lucky. Irene and Felipe have adopted us and are the best grandparents ever."

The two of them moved away from the group a little and sat protected from the sun under some trees.

Virginia felt comfortable with Susana. "I have lost so much that I don't know where to begin to rebuild my life. My parents abandoned me when I left the cult, and now Ricardo has left me forever."

Susana told her, "It's going to take time, and nobody has the answer for you. The answer is inside you. I know this from experience. My God showed me the way, and you will soon find yours. Only you are responsible for your destiny.

You will have your reward, but everything depends on what you expect from life."

Many times, they were interrupted by Alfredo who, with the excuse of offering snacks or drinks, would sit down with them to listen. When he was leaving, he would always use some of Raul's phrases, most often "Never spit into the wind."

Susana said to him, "I don't understand why you're saying that, but I like it. My husband used to say that all the time!"

After he'd gone again, Virginia continued. "My life was very limited when I belonged to my parent's cult, but when we moved to the Country Club, I met people who were not members of the cult, and I learned a lot more about life."

"The cult," she continued, "is like drug addiction, taking control of your life. Luckily, now I have nothing more to do with them. I also started working and have friends my own age, and have experienced many things that I had never had access to before. Religious fanaticism is a disease that destroys the spirit. But despite all this, I need a religion. I want to believe in a God, a merciful God."

Susana said, "From my own experience, I can tell you that when you stop thinking about what you need, that's when you feel a true sense of peace. Many times, you have to listen to your heart and ignore your brain. It's often wrong. Trust your instincts. Bring a purpose to your life and remember that nothing is more important than your inner peace."

Alfredo returned again and then left after a minute or two. They continued talking.

Virginia said, "Thank you for your advice. You are very right. I have already begun to feel that happiness when meeting other people who don't belong to the cult. For a long time, they were the only ones I knew, but by becoming Paola's friend and meeting Mike, Anton, Irene, Felipe, and the others, I feel that there is a hope for the future that I didn't have before."

Susana smiled and said, "When I volunteered at the convent, I had time to meditate and analyze my inner life and the changes that occurred during my life. I had everything: a beautiful family, all the clothes and jewelry I wanted. I worried about my figure constantly. After I'd been at the convent for a while, I began to recognize what was really important for my happiness, and I found that happiness in helping the needy, without expecting anything in return. But the road to happiness is different for everyone. You have to open your heart. It is the only thing you have to do, and that merciful God is going to guide you."

Susana and Virginia hugged each other, enjoying their shared experiences. They joined the rest of the group. They all helped Paola with the final details for dinner.

Raúl was unbearable and kept repeating to Alfredo that at twelve o'clock midnight, during the toast, he was going to say that he was inside of Alfredo. Alfredo was beginning to think that Raúl couldn't be controlled.

Mike and Anton were in charge of decorating the table. It was very artistic, of course, with a separate table set up for the children. While everyone was talking, Valeria approached

Paola, who was with Alfredo. They sat together for a few minutes, resting after their hard work all afternoon. Valeria told her, "I have a surprise. I'm pregnant, and it's a boy!"

"Congratulations!" They got up and kissed each other.

Alfredo had to listen to Raúl. "I can't stand it anymore! This is a torture, my God!"

"Take it easy! Now let's eat. Leave me alone!" he whispered to Raúl.

"Leave me alone" wasn't enough for Raúl. Alfredo separated from the group in order to have some privacy and told Raul, "We need to talk. After having lived so many years together, I have learned a lot from you, and I don't want you to abandon me. I understand your need to touch and kiss your family. I have also learned to love them. From you, I learned everything. What will my life be without you? You taught me to manage my business, how to charm Paola. I became a man by following your advice. If you leave me now, I will wander without any guidance. I'll be lost. If we continue together, through me, you'll be able to continue living close to your family."

Surprisingly, Raúl didn't answer. He listened very carefully. There was no doubt that he loved being flattered. He hadn't really realized the influence he had on Alfredo's life. He didn't say anything at all, but he began to like the idea of staying just as a witness to his family's life.

After dinner everyone sat in the garden and started the fireworks for the children, because they were very tired and they were not going to hang on until midnight.

At twelve o'clock at night, everyone exchanged kisses and hugs.

Susana said she had some news. "I have a gift for my daughters."

Valeria and Maria José came closer, and she took two small boxes from her wallet and opened them. Each one had a diamond ring, and she said to them, "This is the only thing I have kept from my marriage. It was a gift from your father."

This was the moment that Alfredo had feared would cause Raúl to force him to disclose that he was reincarnated and that Raúl was inside him. But surprisingly, Raúl stayed silent, enjoying the moment.

Nobody understood why Alfredo was so excited to hear this news from Susana. They couldn't know that Raúl's silence at this moment assured him of a long life with his counselor, guide, and teacher.

Alfredo concluded by whispering to Raúl, "I'm very happy because today you listened to your heart."

Acknowledgements

Many thanks to my dear friend, Bill Moote, for all his help during the development of this book.

About the Author

Jorge Mazza was born in Buenos Aires. He graduated from University of Buenos Aires Medical School and moved to Ontario, Canada where he practiced academic medicine for almost 40 years.

Jorge was always interested in writing and now in retirement is enjoying writing and this is his first novel